I'LL REMEMBER YOU IN RED

I'LL REMEMBER YOU IN RED

JESSIE GEORGE

For Bryant, with love forever.

1

The Fall

They say it's wrong, but my soul is torn in two when you aren't near.
So, how could it be anything but right?

Smoke flooded my nostrils before the doors of the subway opened. The station's fluorescent lights tried in vain to shine through the haze that had overtaken the crowded train. Murmurs from the crowd bubbled through the silence as a collective panic slowly boiled over. It's human nature to fear the uncontrollable. Our fear keeps us safe. But it also confuses us, bringing out the most primal element in us all.

Firecracker coughs rang out, one after another. The murmuring had grown into a constant buzz, like locusts bursting from the earth. The temperature was rising. Partly, I imagined, from the source of the smoke. But partly because of the nerves seeping through the pores of every soul aboard. Only minutes ago, they had been brave enough to venture into the heart of the city. Now, it smelled like many regretted their choice. I knew what I was getting myself into. We'd all heard the stories about the fires in the streets and the burning Rain.

It was Friday night in New York City, and I was on the Q train heading toward Forty-Second Street. It should have been the height of rush hour, with throngs of people swarming in and out of trains, buses and taxis, coming and going from all directions. I should have been greeted by the smell of stale air, discarded pizza and cleaning solution. All of that had been overtaken by the smoke that was only getting stronger by the second.

Trepidation hung in the air as we all lunged against the slow of the train and heard the siren squeal of the brakes bringing us to our destination. The smoke was nearly blinding now, searing my eyes and hiding the world from my sight. I could barely find the doors to exit, stumbling as I stepped onto the platform. It wasn't until the train left, rushing off with a gust of air momentarily dissipating the haze, that I realized I was the only one who'd been brave enough, or fool enough, to get off the train.

I hurried toward the stairs, then grabbed hold of the railing before my vision blurred once more. I held my shirt up to my nose, wheezing through the cotton in a futile effort to protect my lungs. My eyes and throat burned with every step closer I took. I nearly turned back with each inch I moved forward. I tried to convince myself that once I reached the exit it would be better, that the fresh air would filter out the thick of it. I never could have imagined that it would be worse above ground.

Stepping out of the Times Square subway station is always disorienting. After all that time beneath the surface, with only blank walls and tile floors for miles, you're suddenly assaulted by the flashing lights and boisterous racket of the city's soul. It was easily my least favorite part of this island. Not to mention a constant sore spot in my marriage. Tonight, I found myself wanting nothing more than to be accosted by the familiar.

The smoke was heavier still, though gusts of chilling wind provided momentary relief every few steps. The sound is what I noticed first; a deep, rumbling roar vibrated through the streets. It blanketed every block, dulling my senses. I heard passing snippets of sound as I fumbled through the haze. The sound of crying echoed in and out of focus. I turned my head from side to side, trying to locate the source, hoping to help. It was only after several minutes of search that I realized the crying was coming from all around. Each step I took brought me further from one source and closer to another. Sobs pierced through the veil, but were quickly overtaken by screams, which in turn gave way to moans. I was nearing my destination.

My pace quickened as the smoke dissipated. The roar was getting louder now. The sound rattled my head, sending a painful ringing through my skull. My eyes, scarcely recovered from the sting of the smoke, snapped shut at my first glimpse of light. I held a hand to the sky, shielding my vision barely enough to finally glimpse the horror I had hoped was fiction.

The fire was larger than I ever could have imagined. Larger than any I had seen with my own eyes. Firemen battled against the flames, dousing the blaze with dozens of hoses. If their effort made any difference at all, it was only to keep the trickster flames from spreading to innocent buildings. Tears welled in my eyes but were stolen by the heat before they could escape. There was no way to deny it now. The Fall was here.

A crowd had gathered around the heart of the blaze, encircling it with jeers and taunts. Many had brought tinder to toss into the pits. I pushed forward, squeezing my way through the crowd until the masses were so densely packed that I could not move forward or backward. I was a part of it now. I turned to my left and watched alongside others who had come to witness. I saw the streaks of tears down their faces, washing small slivers of ash and dust away from their skin. Their eyes were swollen from the on-slaught of heat and smoke. Sorrow lined the hearts of all who came to bear witness to what others had intentionally destroyed. Our shared gaze was broken as those around me tilted their heads toward the sky in unison. I turned around, searching for the sight that had stolen their attention until I too saw what the crowd had spotted.

A shimmering, flat object was falling from the sky, launched from one of the high-rise buildings lining the fire. Its gilded casing glinted against the light of the fire as it somersaulted through the air, falling nearly a dozen stories before crashing into the pile. The crowd went silent as we all waited for the inevitable.

After a few moments of roaring silence, someone shouted and pointed to the sky. A rain of color drizzles through the night toward a fiery demise. Portraits, watercolors, tapestries and even jewels rained down on the street below as they were launched from their loving homes. My heart dropped as I watched priceless works sacrificed. As each landed in the flames, they sent a whoosh of sparks into the darkness. It was as mesmerizing as it was devastating. The crowd's volume rose steadily as sparks shot up from the flames. Cheers applauded each death with the conviction of the Romans.

It wasn't until the first scream that we all realized danger was quickly encroaching on us. As more and more art rained down, naturally, some did not reach its intended destination, detouring and striking members of the crowd.

The dense mob moved in synchronized rhythm, swaying back and forth. Inner audience pushed to get away from the center, only to be shoved backward by neighbors doing the same.

I stayed as still as I could, letting the crowd pass me by, taking my chances on the airborne artillery over the stampede. That's when I saw him.

I recognized his fair, shaggy hair in an instant. He too was standing his ground, though it was in a trance rather than intentional inaction. I enjoyed only a few seconds of recognition before I saw an object hurtling on a straight course for where he stood.

"Seth!" I shouted as loudly as my raw throat could muster. I knew it was fruitless, and yet I continued calling as my feet propelled me across the stream of people. I dodged as best I could, mumbling apologies as I crashed into men and women alike. The chaos of the moment was overwhelming as I tried to keep my focus on the moving crowd and the imminent impact.

Seconds stalled as I realized I would never reach him in time. Subconscious reaction took control as my head bowed, and my feet pushed off the ground. I was airborne for no more than a heartbeat before making impact with Seth's torso, slamming us both into the ground. Inches away, where Seth had stood, a frame splintered into hundreds of pieces, shooting shards of wood in all directions, like nails from a gun. Seth and I panted, taking in the worthless mass of the mangled carcass. Weeks ago, this piece would have surely been worth thousands, and yet today it was no better than kindling tossed into the fireplace.

"Hey, Boss." Even in the midst of this horror, a boyish grin spread across his face. I couldn't help but chuckle at what I had always perceived as innocence, but now new to be indignant optimism.

"Save the pleasantries for the office, kid. We've got to get out of here."

We ran for miles. We darted across streets, dodging between brawls around the outskirts of the theater district. We avoided subways and buses, knowing that enclosed spaces weren't safe in such a volatile climate. We approached three taxis, but no one was willing to crawl through the broken streets of the city tonight.

In the end, we walked. We've never spoken about that night, about the turning of the era we both witnessed. We didn't need to. We both understood that the world as we knew it had died that night. There was nothing more to say.

We parted ways when we finally reached East Eightieth Street. Seth trudging on ahead toward his Harlem home.

I thought the impish light of a new day would have brushed the peaks of the skyline by the time I finished the climb to our third-floor apartment. To my surprise, night was still fully positioned on its throne, showing no signs of abdicating.

Tess was by my side instantly as I closed the door to the outside world and fell to my knees. I was sure she could smell my smoke-stained skin from two flights earlier, but she said nothing as she held me close, cradling my head as I wept. I inhaled the sweet relief of her scent until morning threatened to break through enemy lines, illuminating the casualties left from the darkness.

Her skin was speckled with droplets of ash that had fallen from my cheeks. Slowly, she guided me toward running water, washing away the remnants of what I had witnessed. It was a relief to watch the gray water swirl and pool around the drain, though we both knew it was merely symbolic. There was no unseeing the events of that night and there was no going back to the way things were before.

There was only forward toward the looming light of an uncertain dawn.

2

Inevitability

Waterfalls of red, orange, yellow, and green cascaded around us. No one knew it would be the last time we'd ever see them. The trees lost their leaves, and when the spring thawed the earth, all the colors had faded away. Every rosebud, every blade of grass, every singing bluebird had faded to gray.

I stared at the radio, waiting for it to come to life with more updates on the horrors of the world. It stared back in silence, mocking me for my attentiveness. My wife had gifted me the relic for our first anniversary. It pains me to admit that when I first saw its wooden face, I was disappointed. No one uses radios anymore. Hell, no one even listens to the radio anymore, but Tess was beaming with pride, and I couldn't bear to shatter the happiness in her gaze.

"It must be lonely," she said, "working in your studio all day with no one to talk to."

"I don't mind the quiet," I replied absentmindedly before registering how my words might be construed. "But this is a wonderful gift. I'll be glad to use it."

"Killian," she whispered. "It's okay to be honest." Her smile closed into a fine line, twisting at the corner toward the glint in her eye.

I painted my first studio collection while listening to that radio. That collection will always be my favorite, not because it was the first, nor because it sold for enough to pay my studio lease for a whole year. Even now, thinking back on the long nights and countless hours with my brush pressed against canvas, I only remember her. Her spirit flowed through that radio, filling the room with the scent of fresh-cut flowers and summer breeze. Her love became fused with every stroke, in every crevice of those paintings.

She's with me still, even now that the radio has gone silent and the wind turned cold.

I had spent the morning willing a blank canvas to inspire me. It was a futile effort. I knew it even as I stared at the emptiness for hours on end. Still, I'll always regret not trying harder to take advantage of what little time I had left. Instead, my mind reeled through fears of what was to come.

Even in the darkest periods of history, when neighbors turned on neighbors and hatred seeped its way into the hearts of good men, art had survived. I had always believed that art was as integral to society as sunlight was to the fields. Now I knew that I had confused my own needs with those of the whole. The painter was now a dying profession, shriveling under the gaze of a traumatized world. I couldn't blame them. Even I didn't want to witness my art anymore. I feared I never would again.

The moment my life changed was as ordinary as any moment before it. I was watching the clouds go by. I had never taken a lot of time to watch the sky before. Some might call that a silver lining. I called it a tragedy. It was October and there was a storm on the horizon, but still sunlight blazed through the wide windows of my office. The hum of the radiator blanketed the racket of the city streets, calling out for attention even in the current state of the world.

My phone buzzed, startling me out of my trance. I didn't need to look at the screen to know who it was.

"Hey, honey."

I knew that voice anywhere and I couldn't help but smile, even on such a miserable day.

"Hey, babe. How are you?"

The silence on the other end was enough to send chills down my spine. A boulder fell to the pits of my stomach, alerting me that it had finally happened. There was no going back now. A ringing in my ears muffled her response; not that I needed to hear her words to know what was coming.

She sniffled quietly, trying in vain to hold back the tears I was sure were rolling down her cheeks. She let out a meager cry, the pitiful sound snapping me back from the shock. I let out a sigh, not of sorrow, to my surprise, but of relief. The waiting was over. Now it was time to accept the new world.

"Don't worry. I'm on my way."

* * *

I walked up to our third story apartment with two armfuls of Thai takeout. I waddled up the flights of stairs, weighed down by more food than two people should even try to eat. When I finally reached unit 302, I performed a short juggling act as I attempted to maintain my grip on the bags of food while fumbling to get my key in the old, rusty lock. As I shoved the metal into place, I didn't even think to question my actions. No one does anything in this world without a purpose, and love is the purest purpose of them all. We all want to believe that love is the force that drives us. I am guilty of that foolish belief more than anyone. As a child, I convinced myself that I painted for love, to earn the love of a man who would never be proud of his son. Decades later and I was still blind to the truth of why I painted. It wasn't until I succumbed to the blindness that I understood true love never has to be earned.

Had I turned my back on her—running from a result that was inevitable—would it have made any difference? That question would keep me awake in the months following. I grappled with it repeatedly, desperate to go back to that moment and try another way. I know now that this was simply self-inflicted torture. There wasn't a world where I could abandon her. Even now, knowing what I know, I would make the same choice. I would always choose her.

Tess stood atop our kitchen counter, dancing to pulsating music. Although dance was a generous. word She was moving her arms across her body rapidly, her hands in fierce fists, one punching toward the sky, the other firmly fastened around a bottle of sparkling cider. She was bouncing on her bare feet while shaking her head back and forth with such vigor I thought she might give herself a concussion. Her hair was a color of red that mirrored a Louisiana sunset. It was lost somewhere in between scarlet and burnt orange, forever flickering back and forth from roses in springtime bloom to a cherry tree in autumn. She was a flame too beautiful to turn away from.

Her eyes were shut tight. She was fully concentrated on the rhythm of the music, though it was a futile effort. This chaotic display of movement paused only briefly every few beats for her to chug cider straight from the bottle. I took the opportunity to watch her lost in the moment. I wanted to remember her this way.

The music pulsated out, making room for the next musical selection of the evening. She paused from her exertions and took a few deep panting breaths. It was at this moment she first noticed me standing there. Her eyes caught mine and immediately flicked away. Almost instantaneously, they fluttered back, finally realizing she had an audience. She let out a small yelp as the realization startled her out of the musical trance.

"Killian!" she cried. "I didn't see you there. You scared me half to death."

I couldn't help but chuckle. Tess was always lost in her own world. Startling her back to reality was a common occurrence for me.

"I didn't want to disturb you. The rain dance is coming along, although this time of year you might cause a blizzard."

Her eyes closed into slits, and her brows screwed together disapprovingly. She gave me a glare that would send shivers down my spine if I didn't know she was joking. Though, maybe she was trying to summon an ice storm. "Drop the attitude and get your ass up here, Mr. Dance Critic." She beckoned me with the curl of her finger. It might have been cheesy, but that didn't mean I wasn't into it.

I dropped the takeout bags on the floor and leaped onto the counter. Though my heroic hop was closer to an old cat trying to wiggle its way up the bed rather than a graceful Olympic hurdler. I could have sworn that damn counter was shorter than it was. Tess only watched with a bemused smirk as I shimmed my way up to meet her.

"My counter-dancing technique is rustier than I remember."

Another song thudded through the speakers and Tess raised an eyebrow in challenge. "Show me what you got hot shot."

We danced like drunken fools. It was the kind of reckless freedom we would have found years ago, back before we knew each other, back when we were different versions of ourselves. It was freeing to tap back into that side, to let go and let the music guide me. It was made all the better knowing that we were together now, happier and healthy than those old selves ever could have been. By the time we slithered our way to the lukewarm food, we were panting from laughter.

She sat on the floor; her legs crisscrossed in front. One hand held a half-eaten spring roll, the other was communicating with the music, still softly rumbling in the background. Her fingers flicked back and forth, sometimes circling, as if the music had become the conductor and her hand could only follow in its path. Her eyes were closed, not scrunched together as before, but lightly creased crescent moons. Her head bobbed along to the music. She was nodding in absolute agreement with everything Soulja Boy had to say. A stray hair was hanging in front of her face. Every few beats she would let out a puff of air to push it back in place until eventually her bobbing would compel it to fall back in front.

She was impossibly beautiful. Watching her in this state was like sneaking into a theater to watch an explicit movie. I was a boy again. Heart racing from the fear of getting caught but too enticed by the wonders before me to tear my eyes from the view. But the security guard was on the prowl tonight. Tess suddenly stopped her bobbing and opened one eye to stare me down.

"Are you watching me?" A thin smile spread across her lips, almost as if it was daring me to challenge her.

"And if I am?" I replied. Challenge accepted.

Her jaw dropped in theatrical shock. "Didn't your mother ever teach you staring isn't polite? You'd better make it up to me." She pressed her mouth into a tight line and turned her head, crossing her arms in show. There was still a half-eaten spring roll in her grip. Her ruse dropped only for a moment as she threw the rest of it into her mouth and immediately returned to her position, chewing with passion.

I didn't need to be told twice. Tess was not a patient woman, and I did not intend to waste any time. I sprang forward, wrapping my arms around her. She squealed and attempted to wiggle out of my grasp. In a counterattack, I fell backward, taking her with me, until we ended up rolling across the carpet. In that moment, spiraling across our living room, gazing into her eyes as we roared in laughter, I couldn't think of anything better in the world. When momentum rolled us to a stop, I locked eyes with hers above me and kissed her hard. Her hair tumbled down around us in a river of rouge, encompassing me in her perfume.

"Did that make up for my impudence?"

She thought for a moment and languished in a contemplative hum. "Nope. Better try again."

Kissing her melted the world away. Gone were the abandoned spring rolls, gone was the bad music; gone was the Fall closing in around us. I took my opportunity to gain the upper hand, rolling us again until it was me on top. I pinned her arms to the floor, curling her fingers in between mine, and dove back in to leave little kisses across her jawline, trailing up toward her hair. I took a quick detour to nibble on her ear, gently pulling her earring with my teeth. My eyes were closed in concentration, but I heard her breath hitch in her throat, my green light to continue down this path.

"How about we take this after-party to the bedroom?" I whispered in her ear.

Her eyes shot open. Breaking the trance, we had both been under. "No!" she shouted.

I released her arms and sat back hastily, giving her space to sit up and compose herself. "Tess, what's wrong? I thought you were enjoying that."

"I was," she settled for a moment and gave me a quick wink. "Believe me, I was, but I don't want to go into the bedroom yet. If we go in there, then we're going to get tired and fall asleep early. This might be our last night before . . ." She trailed off, hesitant to speak what we both knew. "I don't want it to end early."

She was right. I had gotten caught up in the moment and had completely forgotten about our impending doom. We both sat in silence for a while, considering what to do next instead.

"How about a movie? Anything you want," I suggested.

She smiled at me, and all was right in the world again. "I want to watch *The Wizard of Oz*," she said with a slight giggle.

"Little on the nose, Tess, don't you think?"

"I think it's perfect." Tess always did love a good theme. "I'll get the popcorn," she said, already arising from the floor and walking toward the kitchen.

"Popcorn?" I called behind her, "Tess we haven't even finished dinner yet!" I knew better than to argue with her on popcorn though. She never watched a movie without popcorn, no matter the time of day or how hungry she was. Though wasteful to the takeout, it was immensely comforting to know that despite the chaos around us, some things still hadn't changed. Even if only for tonight.

* * *

"Killian."

A whisper brought me back to consciousness. My eyes blinked open into nothing.

"Killian," Tess hissed.

My mind immediately swam back to the Fall. Had it started? Was she in pain?

"Tess, what's wrong?" I couldn't see her in the dark, but her whimper was unmistakable.

I pulled her close to me, her head was nestled under my chin. She barely made a sound. Her hiccuping tears formed a small stream against my chest. She sniffled and tried to wipe them away before I could notice. Tess had never been one to let me see her cry. Hearing her now caused a dread deep inside me. All I wanted to do was fix it, but there was nothing I could do to stop her tears. I held her tighter, wordlessly whispering to her that I was here, and everything was going to be okay.

Slowly, her tears were dammed back. We laid there silently, listening to only the other's chest rise and fall.

"I'm so scared."

I stroked her hair, kissed the top of her head and reassured her with the only thing I truly knew. "I am too."

Everything was going to change. Our view of the world would be obliterated and reborn into the unknown. I was terrified, but still I held her tight. Her chest rose and fell, slowly calming into its normal rhythm. We fell asleep, holding each other and praying that when we woke, we'd find it was all a horrible dream. We closed our eyes on a perfect world, whose population was only us, but when we woke, that world had vanished as if it had never existed at all.

3

Jester of Misery

We were all in this together. We were never alone all along.

"I've got the latest reports for you." Seth slid the file folder timidly onto the desk behind me. My chair was turned away from him as I watched the world below my fifth-floor studio. The streets bustled with anxious people scurrying around in no true direction. From this bird's-eye view, nothing was different. The world appeared as it always had, but that was the farthest thing from the truth.

It should have been a beautiful day. The last remnants of autumn leaves were gently peeking out from the snow lining the trees of Manhattan. The sky was cloudless and blanketed the early November day. Before, I'd rarely taken in the beauty of nature in all its glory, and now all those lovely sights were only a terrible reminder of how everything had changed. The streets should have been littered with vibrant orange and red leaves drifting off the trees. The emerald grass should have been dusted with white frost, glimmering in the bright rays of this sunny day. The sky should have been a lake of blue, speckled with tufts of wispy white clouds. There were countless things that *should* have been, but it was all gone. The world had lost its color and now everything was just . . . gray.

I suppose that wasn't completely true, as the scientists would say. The Fall had not affected the world around us. Nature was still as beautiful and luminescent as always, but humans had lost the ability to see it. I was rather uninterested in the science behind it all. All I needed to know was that the Fall took our color, and we were never going to get it back. Everything had returned to normal and yet nothing was the same at all. Maybe for other people, accountants and lawyers, and those blessed with mundane jobs that never relied on the subjectivity of others. But where did that leave me?

I was back in my studio, desperately trying to find some inspiration, a spark of anything, when all I could think about was how miserable I was. My self-pity consumed me, snuffing out all possibilities for humor or optimism. I was trapped in this shrinking gray box, expected to go on as if my whole world hadn't been ripped apart. I was a jester in a courtroom, tapping out rhythms and routines for a disgruntled god that cared only to see me writhe. I knew the truth; my career was over. If anyone was lucky enough to make it through the Fall with even a shred of hope, the last thing they wanted was a reminder of what had been lost. That's all I was now—all any of us 'artists' were anymore—an unwanted reminder.

"Boss?" Seth was still standing at my desk, waiting for some reaction from me. Swiveling around to face him, I glanced briefly at the folder he had placed on my desk. I didn't need to review its contents to know what it said.

"Are they any better this week, Seth?" I asked, out of habit rather more than anything else.

Seth glanced down at his shoes and then all around the room, trying not to say what he was going to. He eventually sighed. "They're lighting another fire tonight."

I hadn't been able to bring myself to paint anything since that night. It was the longest I had gone without some spark of inspiration since I was a teenager. Yet, I still couldn't bring myself to cement on canvas what I knew wasn't true. It was too painful to think I would never be able to truly see any of my life's work again. No one would ever see them again, not in the way they were meant to be seen. No one would ever truly see *me* again.

My heart fluttered, thinking about the terror I found in the darkness. Memories of the smoke blistered my throat as I lay awake at night, haunted by that darkness all around me. I knew Seth felt it too. We had witnessed something that even the most hopeful of souls would be tormented by. Not many people get to witness first-hand the ruin of their dreams. I suppose we were lucky in that way. We had seen the truth of the world now, and there was no mistaking that hope had abandoned us all.

I wished I could blame them. The elite in their ivory towers throwing away all evidence of the old world. Except, I know deep down that if I were in their shoes, I'd be doing the same thing. In my darkest moments since the Fall, I imagined chucking out every canvas, paintbrush and palette, joining in their game of merry destruction. The scene plays out in my mind, watching the highlights of my career barrel toward the ground below, shattering into a million pieces. It made me think about things I'd have rather left buried below.

"Sit down for a minute."

I gestured to one of the leather chairs that lined my desk. I had purchased those chairs from a sophisticated uptown store after signing the lease to my studio. I pictured meeting clients and buyers in my office, offering them an elegant chair to sit on, an analogy for the quality of my work. In all honesty, the chairs were as stiff and unforgiving as they were expensive. To add insult, the only person who ever sat in them was Seth.

He slumped down, disgruntled, as he had many times before. Seth was hired as my apprentice under a year ago. The irony of the timing was not lost on either of us. I'd been instantly drawn to the kid; he had a charm and ingenuity about him that's contagious to be around. That's partly why I hired him; he brought a fresh perspective that balanced my own insecurities, not that I'd ever admit that to him. In the days following the fire, we'd bonded. Spending many late hours in the studio, both avoiding going back to a place that was more a holding cell than a home. The more I get to know him, the more Seth reminds me of who I once was. He sees the world for what it could be, full of endless potential.

I might have been his boss in technicality, but truthfully, I was almost intimidated by him. Or maybe it was more that I admired him. I saw potential in the kid and there was a certainty in my core that he was going to succeed. Hell, he'd no doubt end up more successful than me. He was brimming with raw talent but had a lot to learn about the business side of creativity. A reality that I was still becoming accustomed to. Nevertheless, I valued his opinion, and his loyalty had earned him a right to give his insight into our business dealings. Not to mention, I needed the advice.

"What are we doing here?" I asked, candidly.

"Sir?"

"What are we doing here, Seth? We sit in this studio all day trying to paint for a world that doesn't want to see it. What's the point anymore? How do we make anything worthwhile without color? What do we do, Seth? Tell me what you think."

Seth stared at the floor, crafting his words with care. His brow creased and folded as he formulated his thoughts, his feet gently tapping together in a rhythmic melody. Watching him reminded me of a young child trying to figure out the world around him—determined to understand and naively optimistic that he will. When he finally spoke, he did so with care, his words falling gently into the air, cautious but firm.

"Change is a hard thing to swallow. We spend our lives working toward goals and dreams that we have for ourselves. We work and we work and maybe, if we're lucky, we'll achieve those goals. But even then, even if we work hard, it's not enough. Sure, maybe you get that job or meet the girl, but then what? What's next? What happens when happily ever after ends? It's no wonder that hardly anyone ever achieves their goals. Because once you do, what do you do then? Figuring out your dreams is the first half of it; the other half is much harder and much more frightening. We don't want to admit it but change haunts us every day. Nothing is ever permanent. There's always going to be a *what's next?* When you get down to it, why even bother trying in the first place?"

He paused for a moment, lost in the trail of his own words. His eyes told a story that his words did not. I could see a pain in the boy's eyes that I saw in myself. I realized that Seth was far from the naive child that I painted him to be. I selfishly wondered what he had gone through, what dreams he had given away, to instill such youthful wisdom.

"But that's the beauty of it." His solemn stare abruptly changed back to the boyish grin I know so well. "Change may chase us, but we never stop running the race. We can't give up. Yes, people yearn for the way the old world. Yes, it's hard to move on from how everything used to be. But we can't give up. There's still beauty in the world and it's waiting to be rediscovered. And truly, there is no nobler pursuit." He gave a small smile and a shrug, rising from his chair triumphantly. I imagined a trumpeted fanfare playing inside his mind.

I chuckled lightly, shaking my head. The kid never ceased to surprise me. "Have you been talking with my wife? That's something she would say," I retorted.

Seth called over his shoulder as he sauntered toward the door. "I'd say she's a smart lady, Boss. You should go home and talk to her. It's nearly seven o'clock." He gave a short wave, akin to a salute, as he left my office.

He was right. I should go home, but I couldn't bear to face her. The sound of the door clicking closed locked me in with my thoughts. It sounded simple when he said it, and yet, there I was, still staring at a room of empty canvases.

4

Alone Together

*I try to call out, to ask for help, but how can someone help you escape
your own mind? How could I even ask them to?*

I was guided into the studio's gallery room by an invisible force.
I'd had countless memories in this room, both good and bad.
When I first signed my lease for this space, I thought a world of
opportunity had opened. I hosted my first showcase mere weeks
after. I was filled with anticipation and excitement; I was practically giddy. Tess and I were children that first night, running
through the halls, hiding behind corners and squealing. One unin-
tended perk of having your own space was the complete lack of
rules. We ended that night far less clothed than we had when we
began. The memory brought both a twinge of nostalgic pleasure
and present dread.

Nothing had been the same since the Fall. My painting had always been the one aspect of my life that I controlled. It was the
one thing that stuck with me through the addiction, through re-
building of my life: art never left me. Now, I was completely alone.
Tess couldn't understand what the loss meant to me. How could

she? Her world was changed the same as mine, but she didn't *lose* something the way I did. She will never know my hopelessness and for that, I can never forgive her.

I couldn't have anticipated how the Fall would affect me. Logically in my mind, I knew what would happen, but nothing could have prepared me for the profound loss that struck me when that moment finally came. The horrible morning when I awoke to face the world and was greeted with nothing but gray. I'm not ashamed to say that I cried. I cried the whole morning. It was an inescapable grief that could never be rectified. The strength of the emotions terrified me. Despite the assumption of all creatives being deeply in tune with themselves, I was always one to push away my feelings, rather than face them. When my grandfather died, I lashed out at everyone around me. I made mistakes that I am still making amends for. The three-year sobriety chip in my wallet was a constant reminder of that. My track record hadn't improved much since then, because there I was in an empty gallery twiddling my chip, desperate for a hit and avoiding my wife. My sweet wife who had stood by me during my darkest times. My dear wife, whom I loved more than life itself. My *fucking* wife, who would never have to live a life of 'withouts.'

I didn't want to be angry at her. It wasn't her fault. She couldn't have foreseen these recent events any more than I could have and yet, I couldn't help this burning rage toward her. I tried to push the thought from my head. I pushed it deep down into the crevasses that no one dared venture into and channeled it into something else. The stark, emotionless walls of the gallery were still littered with the works I created for my last showcase. The last time they had been seen by the world, they were still beautiful. Now their bleakness mocked me. Their stoic stares laughed at me, taunted me. Open space can give you room to grow, but in the vastness of this empty night, it was only more room to suffocate.

For the next several moments my mind went blank as I stormed into the supply closet and tore through bottles of expensive pigment, effectively rendered useless now. I found the darkest shade I could and ripped a brush from the wall. I gave no thought to my tools as I tore into the paintings along the walls. I slashed and stabbed at them with globs of dark paint; paying no mind to the drips and splatters I left across the floor. I trailed my paintbrush across the wall, not stopping at the canvas, leaving wretched wakes of paint everywhere I turned.

* * *

My body slumped to the floor, panting, while consciousness took back control of my body. How long had it been since I lost myself in my art? I let out a chuckle. I must have looked ridiculous; I certainly felt it. I swatted at a bead of paint along the crease of my forehead and caught a glance at my watch as I did. It was a few minutes past 9:45. I had been here for nearly three hours and yet I would swear only seconds had passed. I steadied myself, reveling in the everlasting numbness. I was spent, physically and emotionally, a husk of myself. I didn't bother with trying to clean up. Along with my many other messes, that was a problem for tomorrow.

I flicked off the lights of the studio and impatiently pushed the elevator button, beckoning it to arrive sooner. I watched as the overhead fluorescent lights clicked off, one by one, edging closer to my position. Watching the darkness grow closer stirred up an oily pit in my stomach. Was there something lurking in the shadows? With a light ping, the doors finally opened, and I hurried into the enclosed box, heaving a sigh of relief. The steely jaws closed in sync with the last of the studio lights flaming out. I laughed at my childishness. No matter how old I get, that fear of the dark never goes away.

I mindlessly stared up at the numbers slowly descending on the front panel of the elevator. 4 . . . 3 . . . 2 . . . My palms were damp. Even through the numbness I'd tried relentlessly to cultivate, I was nervous. As much resentment as I harbored toward my wife, I knew, deep down, I wasn't the only one going through Hell. I shouldn't take my hurt out on her. There was guilt alongside that nervousness too. I knew I'd caused her pain on top of her own grief. Tess once found such joy in the simple colors of everyday life. She asked for sprinkles on her ice cream. She would see a movie based solely on the vibrancy of the poster. Her spirit went gray when the world did. She tried to hold on to the unencumbered energy I loved. She started watching old movies, the kind that were originally black and white. It worked for a while, but I could see how much she missed the way the world used to be.

If I was a better man, I would have sat side-by-side with her in that grief. Instead, I justified my actions. How could I help her when I couldn't help myself? That was a sheepish answer to a selfish problem. If I was honest, I took solace in knowing she was struggling as much as I was. But even that vile comfort wasn't lasting.

The elevator gave another ding, and the doors slid open to reveal the main lobby of my building. As I stepped outside toward the street, it occurred to me that maybe it wasn't the dark I was afraid of, but being trapped with my own thoughts.

* * *

Our apartment was already dark when I slipped through the door. Dishes had piled up in the sink and were overflowing to the counter tops and surrounding tables. I witnessed a graveyard of takeout boxes next to the trash can. The scene in this apartment radiated what I already knew in my heart; we had given up. We had given up on life, on joy and hope. We had given up on each other. The sight stirred something inside me. Was it shame or disgust? Did it matter?

I peeked inside the door to our bedroom and saw my wife curled in a ball on our bed, sound asleep. She was so innocent, clutching our comforter for dear life, her eyebrows scrunched together even in sleep. I skirted around the piles of clothes on the floor and gently sat on the edge of the bed, trying not to wake her. I brushed a curl from her face, letting my hand linger for a moment, taking in the warmth of her skin.

For the first time in weeks, there was a twinge of hope. My outburst at the studio must have loosened the grasp of my emotional blockage. For the first time since my Fall, a tear slid down my cheek. I sat silently in the darkness, watching the love of my life fitfully sleep through watery eyes. With each tear my resentment ebbed. The guilt and shame flowed out in a stampede.

"This is not the life I promised you," I whispered. "I can do better. I must do better."

Those whispered words clung to me. These were more than empty promises ringing soundless in the air. That was a vow I intended to keep. I slipped into bed beside her. I was tired. My grasp on anger and pity was exhausting.

Acceptance rushed in. I was a failure, as a mentor, as an artist, and as a husband. I made a resolute promise to myself. We both deserved more than this pain. Finally, I was ready to do something about it. I lay in the motionless night, staring at the ceiling. I sucked in my last gasp of sorrow and sighed out forgiveness. I forgave Tess for the fault I had placed on her and I forgave the universe for letting this all happen. Most begrudgingly of all, I forgave myself.

5

Sitting in Circles

Maybe that's it. We always want to fix something. We latch on to the hope that whatever we're experiencing, it can be better. It should be better. And we have the power to make it so.

The smell of burnt coffee filled the room. The pervasiveness of the smell might have swelled a sense of nausea in me had the urge to hurl my guts not already been present. The meeting was scheduled for 7 a.m. sharp, but as I checked my watch, I saw it was already 7:05. There were at least a dozen people, myself included, milling about the room. Most were standing near the refreshments table where a dispenser of coffee gurgled out cup after cup of steaming shit. Several boxes of dry donuts and other terrible pastries were scattered across the table, most half-eaten, leaving only least desirable to choose from.

Most already knew one another and were lost in their own conversations, not even realizing that the appointed time had come and gone. I was sitting alone in the circle of chairs, dutifully waiting for everyone to take their places, though there was no apparent haste to do so. I fiddled with the cup in my hand, trying not to show the awkwardness I felt. Faces turned to glance at me from time to time, proving my efforts were in vain. I never thought NA would be so similar to high school, but there I was once again, the weird kid sitting alone at lunch.

My impatience grew with every passing minute. I was supposed to be spending time with Tess. As I lay awake last night, silently berating myself for letting my marriage turn sour, I formulated a grand plan to win her back. I'd taken my first day off work since I bought the studio. I would cook her breakfast in bed and we would spend the day reconnecting. That's what was important, not sitting in a damp basement somewhere along Ninetieth Street, but I knew that this was what Tess would want.

She'd mentioned returning to NA countless times since the Fall, before we stopped speaking altogether. Her voice echoed in my ear, the only thing keeping me glued to my seat instead of walking out of this godforsaken place. She was right, of course. I hadn't attended a meeting in a long time. I didn't need to; with her and the success of my studio, addiction was a distant memory tucked away. A dusty journal within the library of my mind.

Then the Fall changed everything. Today, on the brink of winter, temptation was knocking at the thick wooden doors of the library, beckoning repressed memories to return to the light. I concede that attending the meeting was a good thing. That didn't mean I had to enjoy it.

The clock read 7:12 by the time people finally took their seats and joined the circle I had been sitting in for the last twenty minutes. The familiar sensation of inadequacy came flooding back as every chair in the circle was filled save for the two stationed next to me. Those were left empty.

The conversation had died down to almost a whisper, when the metal doors at the entrance swung open. Bringing with them blinding light and a fresh wafting of New York City sounds.

"Sorry for the delay everyone!" A small man with large round glasses hurriedly shuffled toward the circle and sat with a heavy sigh in the chair to my right. He glanced around the room, nodding and smiling at a few people before turning his gaze on me. His eyes were large, magnified by the strength of his glasses, but held only warmth and genuine interest. I sensed I could trust him even though we'd never spoken.

"There is a new member with us today," the bug-eyed man continued, holding his hand out in front of him. I took it, expecting a handshake, but received a firm clasp with both of his hands as he said, "I'm Edgar. We're glad to have you here." To my surprise, I believed him.

"Does anyone have any objections to our new friend kicking us off today?" Edgar asked the group. Murmurs and head shakes replied as he gestured for me to begin talking.

"Um, hi. I'm Killian and—"

"Hi, Killian," the entire group repeated back to me. I'd attended plenty of NA groups in my time, but the call and response never ceased to catch me off guard.

I tried to shake off the weirdness of having a group of strangers chanting my name, "I'm a painter and I'm only here because my wife asked me to come." A handful of chuckles reverberated through the group at my response. It put me at ease, if only slightly.

"A painter," Edgar exclaimed. "That must be a challenging profession to be in right now."

"You mean because all the color has been drained from the world?" I snapped back.

Edgar only pressed his lips in a tight line and nodded before speaking again. "How long have you been sober, Killian?"

"Three years."

"That's quite an achievement."

"If you say so. I mean, I'm not really an addict. I'm just a guy who made some mistakes a while back. I was addicted, but now I'm not. I got over it. I'm not like—" I stopped myself before indicating that the others were somehow a worse breed of addict than I am. "Anyway, I don't even need to be here, so someone else should go."

I lowered my gaze, trying not to meet anyone's eyes, and especially not Edgar's. I didn't know why I was defensive. I had every intention of coming to this group with an open mind, ready to embrace the process. Yet, as I stared at all the vacant faces watching me, a fire erupted inside. It infuriated me that I was spending my morning here. These people didn't care about me at all. I could have been waking my wife to the smell of coffee and pancakes.

Edgar, for his part, took the cue and prompted another person to begin their sob story. I sat and listened, barely, as they spoke, then another until it all faded together into a dull hum. I hadn't even noticed when the meeting ended and most everyone filed out of the room, back to the sunlight of the streets.

Edgar and I were the only ones left by the time I came out of my trance. His bug eyes were staring at me with an intensity that should have stoked my fire, but how some reason I found comforting.

"I'm sorry. I'm out of practice on how to share with the group, I guess."

"That doesn't bother me."

"Then why are you staring at me?"

"Because you strike me as a man who needs someone to listen."

"Listen to what?"

"You tell me." He smirked and leaned back in his chair casually.

"I'm only here because my wife—"

"You said that. Do you always do what your wife tells you?"

I scoffed, "No. Not always."

"Hmm," he replied, "then why now?"

It wasn't the question I expected him to ask, and I was left dumbfounded for a response. I stuttered and opened my mouth to speak several times, but no words came out.

"You don't have to answer now, but you'll find I'm an excellent listener." He handed me a business card with a name and number printed in solid, stocky letters. "Call me when you're ready."

I stuffed the card into my front pocket and rose from my seat, eager to leave the fire of Edgar's gaze.

"Oh, Killian, one last thing!"

I stopped in my tracks, pinching my eyes shut and hoping with all my might that Edgar would leave and disappear forever.

"Take a couple donuts, will you? They always go to waste unless I bring them home, but my wife will disown me if I show up with more pastry. You understand, don't you?"

I didn't reply but scooped two boxes of half consumed baked goods on my way out the door. I did understand, of course, but he didn't need to know that.

* * *

The coffee was brewing, the dishes were cleaned, the laundry was sorted, and the pancakes were on the stove. It was close to 9:30 by the time the bedroom door creaked open, and I saw Tess's head peak out. She squinted at me through confused eyes, still dazed from her night's sleep. Her hair stuck out in wild angles where she had missed the strands tucked up in a top knot. Her curls were an unruly display, crossing every direction around her face much as I imagined her thoughts at that moment.

"I called Seth to let him know I'm closing the studio today. I thought we could spend some time together," I said. I flipped the first batch of pancakes onto a plate and slid them toward her favorite seat at the table.

She continued her silent squint as she shuffled past me and poured a cup of coffee. She was understandably confused. This was the first day I had taken off in almost three years. I waited for her to say something, anything. She sat down at the table silently, her sleeping shirt falling gracefully onto one shoulder. She hiked up her legs and sat crisscrossed on the chair, cradling her coffee in both hands. She inhaled deeply through the wafting steam and closed her eyes to savor the moment. I took a moment to appreciate her. She was still the most beautiful woman I had ever laid eyes on, even without color.

I plated my own pancakes, complete with a whipped cream smile and two strawberry eyes for a happy face. Seated across from her, I resigned myself to our silent meal and picked up my fork, accepting our nonexistent progress toward reconciliation. As I moved to cut into my stack, she moved her arm across the table and took my hand in hers. It was warm and soft, and it dawned on me that I hadn't touched this hand in far too long. I savored the forgotten familiarity of it, unsure of the next time I might have the chance.

"Are those donuts?"

"They are—" She cut me off, reading my mind as she always does.

"Did you go to a meeting this morning?"

"I did," I replied.

She squeezed my hand gently. "Thank you."

My heart lifted, sending a jolt of hope up through my chest, resulting in a small grin across my cheeks.

"Anything for you." I handed her one of the boxes of doughnuts as I rummaged through the other. "I think there are a few frosted sprinkle ones still left."

Not waiting for a reply, she dug into her stack of pancakes. She paused only to snatch the can of whipped cream and a bottle of syrup from the center of the table. We ate in silence, but for the first time in weeks the silence was welcomed. It was the sound of two people who simply had nothing to say, not of those who were trying to hide what needed to be spoken. We sat there quietly, interjecting only a comment here and there. The pancakes were fluffy. The strawberries were sweet. There was a hint of a smile on both our lips. It may not have been much, but it was a start. The comfortable quiet continued until we were both nearly sick from the sugar. I reached over to store away what was left of breakfast when she grabbed my hand and held it tightly. She held me with her big, beautiful eyes.

"Thank you for going. It means a lot."

For the first time since the Fall, everything was close to normal again. It was my first taste of happiness in this new world. Sweet and subtle and full of hope.

6

Interlude: Part 1

Marc was spending his fourth consecutive evening in an Alphabet City dive bar. In spite of the smell of old beer and even older vomit it was still where he chose to spend most of his nights. The dirt and grime were comforting. It was real. That's what Marc craved.

He had worked another endless day at his father's financial firm, surrounded by facades of faces, all trying to be someone they would never become. It was exhausting pretending to respect those pompous assholes. Each one was less authentic than the next. He was suffocated day in and day out by disingenuous monotony. Each day he'd check the stocks, make some calls, check the stocks again and eventually stumble his way across town to this dump. He'd been coming to this particular bar for years. It was his 'spot' some would say.

He'd never admit it to anyone, but the real reason he kept coming was the hope that his best friend would show up. The one he had met here nearly five years ago. The brother he thought he'd found until Marc fucked it all up. No, he'd never admit that's the reason he still came. He came for the overpriced domestic beers, naturally.

It was nearly 11:30 p.m. when she appeared. He noted the time because it was quite a scene. A girl like her doesn't come around to a place like this. She was tall and slender, yet seductively curvy. She wore leather pants that had to have been painted on her skin. They hugged her every inch, leaving no room for imagination. Marc couldn't help but stare. Her top was a plunging blouse that showed off her best assets graciously. She was illuminated by the neon signs as she walked, a glowing angel from heaven. To Marc she wore a halo made of pure light, although perhaps that was his fifth beer talking.

To his great surprise and pleasure the goddess came up to the bar and sat right next to him. She sat gracefully, crossing one leg over the other and leaning back in her chair. He heard her order a gin over ice with lime but tried not to stare out of politeness. He was a gentleman after all.

He battled to keep his cool as the woman leaned over and asked if he came around here often. That was all the invitation Marc needed to turn on the charm. He told her that he does, in fact, come here often, leaving out that his version of often was nearly every night. The woman was intrigued. She mentioned she was new in town and wanted to see where the locals went. She said she loved a good party and slid a small bag of something that Marc thought was pot across the bar.

With as much charm as he could muster Marc scoffed that weed wasn't much of a party in these woods and he had much better snuff back at his place. The woman gave him an amused smirk. She said she would take him up on that offer, but suggested he try her stash first. She trailed her hand up his thigh, twirling her fingers in a teasing dance. She slipped the small packet into his front pocket, taunting him with her proximity. She smelled of warm cinnamon rolls and early morning coffee. Her scent intoxicated him. But then again, maybe that was beer number six talking. She smirked at him, her full lips curling into a demure grin. Marc was nothing but a gentleman, so he did what the woman said and ordered them a cab back to his place. It was the polite thing to do after all.

* * *

When Marc woke up the next morning, he wasn't sure if he had dreamed the previous night or not. Many of his nights blended into dreams these days and what he thought he remembered was too bizarre to be true. He remembered arriving back to his apartment, the goddess trailing behind him. He poured them some drinks. He even broke out a special bottle of gin. This bottle was infused with butterfly pea blossom giving it a vibrant purple hue. The gesture was thoughtful though useless in the current climate, it wasn't as if either of them could see the color anymore, but still the name Empress seemed fitting for his date.

They danced around the highlight of the evening with small talk about work. She was in town for an art show. She was a gallery owner scouting an up-and-coming artist. Marc reminisced fondly about his old friend Killian who was a successful painter with a studio not far away in Soho. The woman asked if they should invite this old friend, because, in her words, it's hardly a party without at least three. While Marc agreed with the sentiment, he knew two key things the woman did not: One, with Killian present there was no chance Marc would get laid. Two, Killian wasn't any fun to party with these days. He told the woman as much but left out the part where Marc and Killian hadn't spoken in years. For tonight, he would remain the gentleman he wished he truly was.

The Empress, as he decided to call her, pulled her stash from his front pocket and began rolling two thin joints. He was willing to humor the naive child. A simple stash of weed wasn't nearly enough to get him fucked up these days. He thought about the coke hidden in his bedroom, a spot of convenience in more ways than one. As her fingers deftly folded her devilish tongue swiped across the paper, she murmured what a shame it was that his friend couldn't join them. Marc assured her they would have plenty of fun alone.

The Empress only smiled and shrugged her shoulders. Dismissively, she ran her thumb along his lower lip. With a practiced, gentle pull she parted his lips. Marc leaned forward in anticipation but in an instant the touch of her skin was replaced by the joint. Naive she may be, but undeniably skilled. She lit the end and watched with eager delight as Marc took his first hit. That's when things started to get strange.

Marc's mind flooded with confusion as the world around him rolled with a kaleidoscope of colors. Images contorted and folded in on each other. Rolling hills of vibrancy crashed through waves of the mundane. Marc watched with terrified delight as the Empress's eyes slowly mutated to match the color of the smoldering joint. Her beauty gave him a singular focus in a moment of overwhelming chaos. Her long blonde hair gleamed, and her halo sang brightly in the moonlight. Maybe it was he who was naive child all along and she the enlightened one.

That was the last thing he remembered. He awoke in his bed fully clothed, to his dismay. The Empress was nowhere to be found. It had to be a dream. It had to be, except . . . he turned toward his bedside table and saw the small bag still sitting there. Its presence wasn't proof enough though. Marc found some rolling papers stashed in the drawer and lit a joint, needing to prove to himself that the woman with bleeding eyes wasn't a dream after all.

7

Chance

Can you ever get anything for nothing? There's always a price, a promise, a sacrifice. To get one, you must give up the other. Why is the exchange for happiness, happiness? It's a trap. A game. There is no win or lose, there is only the game.

I do love him, though. I do.

I had a new lease on life. Tess had given me a second chance. As small as it may be, I knew that there was still a glimmer of hope that I could win her back. When her eyes met mine, it was as if I had come alive again after months of hibernation. I was practically skipping down the streets of New York. I rounded each corner with heightened anticipation. The concrete sidewalks seemed to bounce with every step I took. The crisp air filled my lungs with excitement, and the sky was an incredulous shade of . . . gray.

In my elation I had momentarily forgotten the cause of all my grief, and now it was all too eagerly flooding back to me. The grin fell from my face as I stood on the edge of the street, staring up into the sky. It was 7:30 a.m. and there wasn't a cloud to be seen.

Last year at this time, even six months ago, I would have been seeing the sunrise burst into the airiest shade of blue; but now, all I see is gray. My stride turned somber for the remainder of my commute. I trotted on in a daze, overwhelmed by my jolt back to reality. By the time I reached the doors of the building lobby, I had completely forgotten about yesterday's pancakes and whipped cream and her smile.

I punched the floor of my office into the panel and hunched back against the walls of the elevator. There was one other man in the elevator with me and, according to the glowing number 4, he was heading to the floor right below mine. He held his newspaper close to his face, close enough that I wasn't sure he could even read anything. His wool peacoat was heavy for the year's mild winter, and the sweat lining his brow agreed with me. He had a large leather duffle bag to his side, which I assumed was filled with gym clothes. There was a small equipment space in the basement of this building, which many people frequented on their lunch break.

My examination of the stranger ended abruptly with the chime of the elevator doors. His floor had arrived, and he swiftly tucked away his newspaper, grabbed hold of his bag, and left the elevator. This wasn't an unusual encounter in any specific way, and yet something about his presence was unsettling. There was a buzz in the air as if something important had happened. What it was I had no clue. I watched him go and only after he walked away did I notice the small dime bag left where he had been standing. The man must have dropped it.

I tried to hold the doors and call out to him, but the elevator beat me to it and lifted me to the next floor. I bent down to inspect the small sample left behind. It was a clear plastic bag about the size of my palm. Enclosed in it was what I guessed to be marijuana. I chuckled in surprise. His strange demeanor suddenly made sense. The elevator dinged again, this time at my destination. I instinctively stuffed the bag in my pocket as the doors opened to the gallery.

I hadn't touched anything stronger than aspirin since the day I met Tess three years ago. She was my shining light in the darkest period of my life. I often wished I had met her somewhere outside of rehab. I wished a lot of things were different about that period of my life, but I've never regretted meeting her. My love for her on that day, and every day since, blinded me to any past vices. When glimpses of my past did resurface, it felt as if I was remembering scenes from a movie, the struggles of someone else, not my own.

Getting sober hadn't been easy. Beyond the chills and the headaches and painful aching of desire, the most difficult symptom to cope with was the fear of losing my career. I had risen to prominence in the art world quite suddenly. A 'right place, right time' kind of thing. Of course, I was also using. I feared that would all go away in sobriety, but Tess helped me see that my artistic value didn't come from any substance; it came from within. She had always seen through to the real me, even when I get lost within myself.

I walked with urgency to my office, rolling the bag over and over in my pocket as I walked. Having it in my presence was almost more exhilarating than any high. My hands trembled slightly as I swiped my key card against my office door. Closing it swiftly behind me and slumping down against the wall. As I sat there on the floor, I brought out the bag again. I held it with both hands in front of my face. My mind played tricks on me, telling me I deserved a reprieve after all I'd been through. It told lies, fueled by old habits. I pictured Tess's smile and the small progress we'd made toward repairing our relationship. That was the truth I wanted to focus on.

A knock on my door interrupted my internal ramblings. I hastily stuffed the small bag into my back pocket before calling out. "Come in!"

"I've got the daily reports for you."

"Thank you, Seth. You can set them here on my desk. How was your day off?" I inquired, eager to draw attention away from myself.

"Oh, you know, the usual. Evidently not as interesting as yours." He trailed off, staring quizzically toward the gallery.

For a split second, I thought he somehow knew about my elevator run-in. I had completely forgotten about my chaotic paint session two nights before.

"Oh that." I chuckled anxiously, letting go of my pent-up nerves. "I got carried away the other night. I was about to clean it up."

"Hold it right there, Boss. Don't you worry about it!" Seth stepped in front of me before I could get past my desk. "I'll take care of it. That's what I'm here for, isn't it?"

He made a fair point. He was my assistant, even if I rarely thought of him in that way. "All right. Knock yourself out, kid. You can chuck everything. No point in keeping that mess."

"Are you sure? I think they're great." I saw him peering back into the gallery, quietly pondering the destroyed canvases. He wasn't completely wrong. In the light of day, my chaotic whirlwind of anger and despair hinted at a certain truth. They were certainly the most intimate things I had painted in some time. Too bad authenticity doesn't sell.

"Take them if you want them, then. It doesn't matter to me. Hey, want to grab lunch at that little bodega down in Chinatown today?" I inquired, changing the subject.

Seth replied, his concentration broken from the gallery, but clearly still distracted by whatever thoughts were running through his curious mind. "Uh, no. Not today. I'm meeting someone. How about tomorrow?"

"Sure thing." The door clicked closed before I had even finished my sentence. Seth was certainly enamored by those paintings. Come to think of it, he was acting peculiar this morning. I wondered if something else was on his mind. It occurred to me that I didn't know much about Seth's personal life. We talked often about his schooling and his hometown and his ambitions. The kid could be a real chatterbox when he wanted to be. But we rarely discussed his daily life here in New York. I could list the names of almost every one of his cousins from back home, but not a single one of his friends in the city. Did he even have any? My curiosity nagged at me to pry more about his social life the next time it came up.

The rest of the morning flew by in a blur. Rows of negative numbers lined the accounting books and merged with stacks of reports for nearly nonexistent online sales. I dreamed of better days, back when this studio was a success. Those days had been a mere few months ago, but those months might as well have been a lifetime. The studio had been consistently bringing in good returns for almost a year now. I had even thought about opening a second location before everything changed. Business had been so good, in fact, that I hardly had any time to paint myself anymore. Most of my time was spent managing the day-to-day functions of the gallery.

When I first purchased this space, I had always imagined I would spend most of my time in the studio. Painting for private owners and sending my extra work to the gallery for purchase here and there. But as time evolved, I was receiving more commissions than I could keep up with, let alone stock the gallery. It was Tess's idea to bring in young, up-and-coming talent to fill the gallery, letting me focus solely on commissions. A brilliant idea at that.

That's how I first met Seth. I had approached Columbia in search of some grad students, and he was at the top of their list. We met for a brief consultation, and the rest was history. Eventually, the gallery became successful enough, I stopped taking on commissions altogether to spend more time there. Funny how things change. Selling prints and digital copies of my past works in the online store was the only place any of my original art lived now. I could blame the Fall as much as I wanted, but if I was honest with myself, I hadn't painted anything new in quite some time. That was a hard truth to swallow.

It was almost 1:30 before I heeded the call of my grumbling stomach. Not eager to spend too much time away from my desk, I opted for a halal cart across the street. Armed with a chicken gyro and an energy drink, I stepped back into the building elevator only ten minutes after departing.

As I was in the elevator back up, it dawned on me that the result of this morning's run-in was still in my pocket. I should have tossed it while I was waiting for my food but had completely forgotten. The thought of returning it to its owner briefly crossed my mind before realizing that would be nearly impossible. I could barely remember what the man looked like, and I certainly did not need to stick my nose into his business. After all, I couldn't leave it for him at the front desk. In fact, there might not even be a front desk to leave it with. To my knowledge, the fourth floor had been vacant for over a year. I didn't remember a new company moving in, though I supposed it was easy to miss things in the midst of a global crisis. To my surprise, the elevator stopped at four and the doors opened to a familiar face; it was Seth.

"Oh, hey, Boss," Seth choked out, obviously startled. I tried to peer behind him to see what had taken over the floor but saw only a glimpse of darkness before the doors closed behind him. He stepped inside the elevator and was instantly chattering a mile a minute. "I was coming back from lunch and must have accidentally hit the wrong floor number. You know me, head always in the clouds." He chuckled exaggeratedly.

He was definitely acting strange. I gave him a questioning glance, prodding for information.

He let out a sigh and his fake, overly excited smile dropped. "All right, you got me." He sighed dejectedly.

My curiosity piqued. I had no idea what I had inadvertently uncovered.

"I did hit the wrong button, but it was because I was distracted trying to solve this stupid daily Sudoku puzzle in the paper. I walked halfway onto the floor before realizing it was completely empty. None of the overhead lights were on, and I got spooked. I ran back to the elevator and was pressing the button like a lunatic when you showed up."

We both laughed at his recounted tale. That sounded more like the Seth I knew. Though I teased him about being afraid of the dark, I'd had a similar experience the other night. The building did get eerie in the dark. I couldn't blame him.

"Wait, you mean there's nothing on the fourth floor?" I asked.

"Not unless you count empty filing cabinets and boxes of dusty office supplies. I poked my head into one of the corner offices and saw nothing at all. Not even a desk, just an old plastic chair mat," he replied.

"There was a man in the elevator this morning who got off there. I wonder what he was doing."

Seth shrugged, clearly not as intrigued by the mystery man as I was. "Maybe he was a contractor inspecting the space for a new lease." He was already back to fixating on his Sudoku.

I had a nagging feeling that wasn't true, but I agreed anyway, if only to try to convince myself. "Yeah, I'm sure that's it."

8

Little Wins, Bigger Losses

Nothing is ever perfect. As much as we want it to be, there's always something to pick at. A loose thread that you can't help yourself from pulling on That little something is always present. It's in the back of your mind, constantly questioning you.

"What if . . . ?"

By the time 5:05 p.m. rolled around, I was ready to bolt out the door. For the first time in weeks, I wanted to go home.

I caught Seth's eye as I left. He gave me a chuckle and a smile as he sat back in his chair and turned two thumbs up toward the sky. I returned his cheeky enthusiasm with a wink. I really liked that kid.

I was bouncing with an unfamiliar energy as I left the towering glass building that held my workspace. I wanted to keep the progress from yesterday going, with a show of good faith that I had truly turned a corner. Flowers would have been perfect. Tess loved fresh flowers and how they always lit up the room. Their naturally vibrant colors always brightened my mood too. Tess's favorites were always marigolds. She said they reminded her of sponges. I remember it sounded strange when she said it the first time.

"Sponges?" I asked.

"Sponges," she replied, "you know those organic sea sponges? The ones you use for painting or taking a fancy shower. I want to pluck them off the stem and sponge the sky."

She would always say crazy things. Things that if anyone else had said them, you'd think they were absolutely loony. But when she said it, her eyes lit up, and a small smile crept across her face. She'd stare at the clouds, lost in her own version of how the world could be. I always wanted to be a part of that world she lived in, the one where it was possible to sponge the sky.

I wish I had bought her more flowers when I had the chance. I racked my mind trying to think of something to substitute the marigolds. I stopped short and realized the answer was staring me right in the face. There was a small Italian bakery a few blocks from our apartment that made the most beautiful chocolate roses. They may not have been sponges, but they would have to do.

* * *

I walked through the door of our apartment at 5:55 with a bundle of groceries and two chocolate roses. This was the earliest I had been home in months, and the surprise on Tess's face confirmed the fact. She assessed me up and down, searching for a reason behind my sudden change in mood.

"Our anniversary isn't for months," she said wryly, hardly glancing away from the book in her hand to give me a side eyed glance. She didn't rise from her seat on the couch as I struggled with the heavy bags in each arm.

"I know, Tess. I wanted to do something special. I thought we could make your favorite tonight. You know, how we used to? I miss cooking with you."

"Do you, Killian?" Her harsh tone took me back. Was she determined to undermine my attempt at amends? What happened to yesterday's smile?

She shut her book with a clap. "Yesterday was nice and all, but don't think it can erase the last few weeks. Some pancakes and an NA meeting won't make up for shutting me out for weeks."

She was right, of course, but my temper took over and I went on the offensive. "I'm not the only one to blame here. You stopped talking too, stopped communicating, stopped letting me help you!"

She was standing now, the book falling to the floor as her arms knocked it from her lap. "And do you know why I stopped talking to you, Killian?" she snapped back at me. "Did you ever think for a minute that maybe you had something to do with that? I know you blame me. I know you blame me for taking it all away from you. It's my fault and I can feel you thinking it the minute I open my mouth and there's nothing I can do to fix it."

She had tears streaming down her face now. She sat back down, wiping the droplets from her face, staring anywhere but at me. I set down the groceries and walked toward her. She was sniffling into her sleeve and avoiding my eyes with everything she had in her. I knelt down to meet her, wiping a tear from her cheek. Holding her hands, I gazed up at her until she finally faced me, but her eyes were still fixed on my shoes.

"I'm so sorry," I said softly. "I want to move past this. I miss you. I miss us. Whatever happened in the past, let's leave it there. All I want is to move forward with you."

It was the truth. I knew I had hurt her but hearing her say it was the confirmation I needed to know that I was finally back on the right track.

"I want that too." Her eyes finally fluttered up to meet mine. She had the most beautiful eyes, even when they were clouded by the tears I caused.

She watched intently as I lifted her hand gently and gave it a kiss. Her eyes traveled up from my lips to meet my gaze and there was that smile again. The one that could melt my heart in even the coldest of arguments, the one I would do anything to keep on her face.

"Now, how about some dinner?" I planted a light peck on her lips before rising up and turning toward the kitchen.

"Killian, what is that?" I heard her ask behind me.

I turned to follow her extended finger, pointing to the corner of the little plastic bag I had found in the elevator this morning peeking out from my back pocket.

I removed it from my pocket and showed it to her, hoping she would take my candor as a sign of good faith. "Oh, Tess, that's nothing. Some guy in the elevator this morning dropped it and I meant to toss it. I completely forgot it was in my pocket. Truly, it's nothing." I was hoping she could hear the honesty in my voice.

Instead, she snapped, taking back the tone of the argument I thought we had ended. "Seriously, Killian? You want me to believe that some guy in the elevator happened to drop a bag of weed and conveniently didn't notice it? God, I'm such an idiot." She closed her eyes and shook her head, disagreeing with my silence. "I knew something was up. I knew all these kind gestures couldn't come from the goodness of your heart. You're using again!"

I tried to grab her arm to stop her tyrannical spiral, to try to convince her I was telling the truth. "Tess, wait, that's not what this is. I meant what I said."

"And what about the meeting, huh? Was that all a big lie, too?"

"Tess, stop. I'm telling you the truth. You have to believe me."

"No, I don't believe you Killian. For three years I've begged you to go to meetings, to find a sponsor, but no, you always convince me that you have it under control. You let me believe that you were past all this. How could I have been so stupid? I mean, I get it, things didn't go your way and you're sad." Her voice turned to mockery, and she gave an over dramatized frown. "But news flash, Killian, the Fall was hard on all of us. You don't think I'm sad too? That I've wanted to burn everything to the ground and leave the past behind?"

Her face was wet with tears; her cheeks were raw and puffy. She pulled in a ragged gasp, trembling with the strength of her anger. "You need to get your shit together and stop acting like a fucking child." She threw the little plastic bag to the floor and stormed past me, slamming the door to the bedroom.

Rage boiled inside me. I turned toward the groceries in the kitchen, and I slid my arm across the counter, sending all the ingredients flying to the floor. My eye caught the chocolate roses, and I threw them against the wall, letting out a grunt of anger. I was more hurt than angry, but I was all too eager to let the anger take control, rather than dealing with the betrayal that stung my eyes. I couldn't believe she thought I would start using again. I scoffed aloud at myself. I was a fool for thinking she would be proud of me for resisting this temptation. She didn't understand, *couldn't*; I'd always feared she had harbored some prejudice against me for my past struggles. I never wanted to admit that my own wife saw me as an addict first and husband second. Now it was the only thought in my mind, repeating over and over.

The little bag was still lying there on the floor of the living room. I stared at it, seething. Two could play in this game. I picked up the bag, letting out a loud, showy groan as I slammed the door to the apartment. As I huffed down the flights of stairs, I wasn't quite sure where I was going. I needed to disappear from here, to go somewhere safe and free from this unwarranted prosecution. I pounded my feet down on each step, trying to take my frustration out on the concrete below me.

I blindly stomped through several blocks. Only slowing briefly to realize that I was, in fact, acting childish, but I let that self-revelation fuel my rage once more. She didn't get to be right when she was the one in the wrong. I turned left and right, paying no attention to my surroundings. It had been almost twenty minutes when I found myself in front of a corner convenience store. Still fuming, I walked inside. I slammed down a ten-dollar bill and requested a pack of rolling papers.

"Keep the change."

As I left the store, I rounded the corner, searching for an alleyway to roll a joint. I didn't know why I was doing what I was doing, but the muscle memory in my fingers swiftly did the work for me. The joint fit in the crook of my fingers perfectly, as if it was made to be there. The familiar sensation sent waves of memory through my body. I sighed, staring down at the joint, wondering what the hell I was doing. Would I throw away three years of sobriety because of a stupid fight with my wife?

I glanced toward the sky, searching for answers. The sun was descending slowly, providing convenient shadows to hide my shameful actions. I scoffed. Of course it was sunset, another dirty reminder that everything had changed. The sky above me was a patchy mess of gray, dark gray, and even darker gray. Gray, all the time, everywhere. It was maddening.

All the rage, betrayal and hopelessness I'd experienced over the last few months reached a tipping point. I wanted to scream, letting loose my wild, pent-up frustration. My heart rate quickened, lungs heaving in and out, trying to keep at bay the panic that was rising within me.

The world was closing in, the walls of the alleys scraped along the ground, inching closer toward me with every breath I took. I couldn't think clearly. Thoughts of the past days and months scrambled together in my mind's eye. Flashing images of Tess, of the studio, of the last sunset I ever saw.

I pulled out the lighter I still kept in habit. I flicked it open and stared at the flame as the rolled joint sat in the corner of my lips, ready for action. I took no moment of reflection. My mind was a numb void as I lit the end of my blunt and took my first hit in three years.

9

Kaleidoscope

So, I watch from the shadows. But the shadows aren't your friends.
The shadows hide their own secrets.
The shadows won't tell you, you are not alone in their darkness.

One hit was all it took. From the moment the smoke entered my lungs, it became overwhelmingly clear that this was not any high I had experienced before. This was something entirely new. In an instant, my dark, dreary world was flooded with the sensation of color. Everything I lost in the Fall was returned.

Vibrant shades of violet and blue weaving through bright oranges and yellows. A river of radiance swirling around everyone and everything in sight. The sky above me, once muted in grays, was filled with the colors I thought were gone forever. Streaks of paint colored the sky. I was a child again and the world was suddenly a new playground to explore. Everything was interconnected in a mosaic of natural beauty. There was wonder in the world again.

I was so taken with the miracle before me, I almost didn't notice: The world I was seeing was not the world I left behind. Something was wrong. The sights were familiar, yet completely new. Could I really have forgotten the iridescence of the world that quickly? It had been only weeks without color, but everything appeared out of place.

No, that wasn't quite it. A longer examination of the sights around me and I realized what I didn't recognize were the colors themselves. I wandered aimlessly, inspecting each new vision before my eyes. I slowly pieced together what my brain was furiously trying to process. The answer I arrived at was too fantastic to be true, and yet the evidence was right before my eyes. This drug had allowed me to see beyond the spectrum I had previously known. New mixes of hues and shades played together in an intricate orchestra. Bursts of neon staccato were paired with legato tones, an elegant mix of light and dark. I watched the colors in the sky swirl in a river of pigment.

My mind was humming with the revelation. This drug had opened a door I didn't think was possible. I had given up on ever seeing the world in full vibrancy again, how quickly I had given up, but now I held the key! My mind raced through the door of opportunity. This meager roll had single-handedly turned my life around. I was George Bailey, and it truly was a wonderful life.

I wandered, lost in the elation of the moment. The sky above me swirled with colors, each one seamlessly blending into the next. Vibrant motions covered the sky, swirls and stripes and valleys and hills. It was beautiful. Not only had color been returned to me, but now the world fluttered with rhythmic motility. Each corner I turned was more beautiful than the last. Simple city streets and sidewalks were renewed with each step. Best of all, I was in control of this new world. It was more intoxicating than any high I'd experienced before.

I glanced up at some familiar street graffiti. It was a sight I had seen all too many times before, never paying much attention to it, and paying even less attention after the Fall. It was easy to ignore the noise of simple street art in a city overcrowded with aspiring artists. I had walked past this mural dozens of times before, but this time, I stopped and stared in astonishment. As I watched the letters and shapes warp around themselves, the painting was brought to life, moving in its own rhythm, alive from within. The sentiment of the design remained, but now it had new life, a beating heart of its own.

Eventually, my legs carried me to a long-forgotten corner of my little world. I found myself at the waterfront, the East River staring back at me in matching surprise and awe. I hadn't been here in months.

When Tess and I first moved to our apartment, we thought we were the luckiest people in Manhattan. 'A waterfront park a few blocks from our front door!' Back before the gallery took off, that type of luxury was far out of reach. Yet we had managed to secure a little slice of paradise steps from this quiet oasis. Benches lined the walkway, looking out over the water into Brooklyn and Queens. Flower boxes stuffed with artificial garland lined the path, carving out secluded patches of snowy grass perfect for hiding from the whistling wind.

It was nearly dark now, the last glimmers of light holding onto the sky with all their might. My eyes watered as I watched the faint glow of purples, pinks and oranges quiet to a whisper as the evening sun grew dimmer. The lights of the city were already in full glow, illuminating the sky in harmony with the setting sun. As the sun fell below the horizon line, my color high faded too.

The walkway was mostly empty, save for a few couples enjoying the water and each other's company. They held hands and huddled in close. The December chill was frigid but being young and in love protects against such frivolous things as weather. Now that the sun had set, some gathered their things and walked off into the night. I imagined them off to a restaurant for a romantic evening, or maybe back home to warm up. Some remained, nursing a cup of coffee, lost in conversation. I remember a time when Tess and I would have been out here on a night like this. Back when we thought this small park was a gift just for us.

The thought of her crept into my mind. A gentle whisper that mellowed the elation burning inside me. The whisper was a fire that crackled with the premonition that, at all costs, I must keep this miracle a secret. I wanted to plunge headfirst into the icy waters of uncertainty, but the fire coolly reminded me none of this could happen. None of this could happen because there was one person who would fundamentally disapprove. One person who would see only danger and threat where I saw wonder and possibility. One person who I could not bear to disappoint, not again.

I returned to the apartment and quietly paced up the three flights of stairs. Tess was the one who guided me through this journey to sobriety. She was there for me during every sleepless night and every agonizing day. How could I explain to her that all of that was . . . gone? How could I tell her that she was right?

When I reached the door, it taunted me with its simplicity. On the other side of that thin piece of wood was the person I promised my life to, the person I was most afraid of disappointing. With a heavy sigh, I turned the lock and entered the room. I was met with surprise as I saw Tess on the couch in front of me. She was tucked under a blanket with a cup of tea in her hands. When her eyes met mine, she immediately set down her mug and walked toward me. I braced for the sting of her words.

She sighed at me and gently took hold of my hands. "I'm sorry." Her eyes welled with tears as she spoke. "I should have believed you. I jumped to a conclusion without listening to your explanation. I trust you, Killian, and if you say that you're still clean, then I believe you."

To say I was surprised by her reaction was an understatement. My wife was many wonderful things, but mellow-tempered was not usually one. Her understanding worsened my guilt. I had been furious with her, to the point I wanted to spite her and ruin all the work we had accomplished. It was clear that the small bag in my pocket did not contain weed as she had accused me of, but I didn't know that when I lit the joint. I had every intention of washing three years of sobriety down the drain. It was only by a happy accident that I found something better.

Her eyes brimmed with honesty and compassion. It overwhelmed me. The candor I had worked up the confidence for was falling further and further down my throat, back into secret. I was going to come clean and tell her the truth. That was the plan. But gazing into her eyes I saw the man she wanted me to be. A man who was trustworthy, who was working through his problems and striving for self-improvement. She saw a man she believed was still sober. I wanted to be worthy of her, to be the man she believed in. So, I lied.

"Thank you, Tess, and I'm sorry too. I should have told you everything the moment I walked through the door." I handed over the small bag. My eyes, almost too intently, watched the miracle substance leave my hands. I prayed she didn't follow my iron stare.

Her fingers daintily pinched the edge of the bag as she held it up to inspect it. She opened it up and gave a faint sniff of the contents. She chuckled lightly, "You're right. It's definitely not weed. I wonder why someone put it in a dime bag." She tossed the bag in her hand a few times. "Wanna toss it?"

She gave me one of those cheeky smiles, the ones that always get us into trouble. I couldn't say no to that smile. Not when it was inviting me back into its warm embrace. So, again, I lied.

"Yes, yes I do." I stepped on the foot of the trashcan to open the lid and watched her toss in the bag. The magical substance fell into a pit of darkness.

* * *

It was 3:00 a.m. and I couldn't sleep. How could I while knowing that the answer to all my problems was waiting patiently on the other side of my bedroom door?

I rolled over again.

I had spent the rest of the evening sneaking glances at the trashcan. I should have been fully engaged in my conversation with Tess. We were finally talking again, finally laughing again, but all I could think of was the magic I had experienced earlier. I agonized over the contents of that bag and the powers they held, flinching when Tess scraped her unfinished food into the canister. I could hardly bear it.

I rolled over again.

I wanted to be a better man than this, the man that she believed I was. I wished I was strong enough to let it go and simply be happy with this life. Why couldn't I be happy with what I had? I'd always valued the fire inside me, the one that pushed me toward perfection in every aspect of my life, but tonight I prayed to be a different man.

She would never understand how that small bag could change our lives. I was not going to give up on this. There was no turning back now, even if that meant I had to sacrifice the progress we had made. I would not give up my career when the answer was staring me right in the face. If she truly loved me, she wouldn't ask me to.

Tess lay blissfully asleep to my right. I avoided glancing at her, knowing if I did the guilt would overwhelm me. I envied the ease with which she lived her life. She never experienced the insecurity and passion I was constantly plagued with. If I followed through on my urges, I'd be turning my back on her loyalty, betraying any faith she ever had in me. And yet, if I was honest with myself, I had already chosen my path.

As much as I prayed in those restless hours, I was still the same man I had always been. The one who valued his career over everything, even, I feared, over her. I chose to storm out of our apartment, to flick open my lighter and put that joint to my mouth. My sobriety was a distant dream due to the choices I made, the choices I was continuing to make. My restlessness was not born of indecision, because, in truth, I had already chosen to betray her.

I let go of the turmoil inside me. I no longer wrestled with the choice I was about to make, because I had already made it. This recognition was easier to accept than uncertainty. Acknowledging I was a fuck-up was far easier than trying to prove I wasn't. I rose from bed and padded over to the bedroom door, careful to avoid the creaks of that old apartment's floorboards. I opened the door and set my sights on my prize. My body was no longer listening to my mind, though it screamed, in vain, trying to wake me from my trance. I opened the lid to the trash, turning my head from the sight as I sifted through food scraps to remove the small plastic bag. I plucked it from the pile and held it to the moonlight. A calm washed over me. I took it as a sign that the path I had chosen was meant to be, some cosmic intervention leading me toward my deserved life.

I needed to find more. The small quantity I had wouldn't last me more than a handful more hits, much less another full roll. It wasn't enough. I needed to track down that mystery man, the one from the elevator. Whatever this was, I needed to be part of it. I didn't know how I would find him. I didn't even know how any of this was possible, but the how wasn't important. I had never been held down by such nuances before, I certainly wasn't going to start now.

I tucked the bag into my briefcase, safely out of sight. I washed my hands and returned to the bedroom, slipped into bed and rolled over to hold my wife tight.

She nuzzled into my arms and whispered softly, "Everything okay?"

"Everything's fine," I whispered back.

She smiled lightly and tucked her head closer into my chest. I held her close. For the first time I believed the words when I said them, because now there was hope, and tomorrow I would forge a new happy ending.

10

Moon Landing

*The rain did not soothe her. The rain reminded her of being alone.
Of the days when she would stare out her window, willing someone to
appear out of the mist.*

No one ever did.

The small bag and its compelling contents sat in the top drawer of my desk all morning. It haunted me as I answered the phone, drank coffee and reviewed our accounts. It burned itself into my skull, stealing my attention away from even the simplest tasks. I was cleaning up the second cup of overflowed coffee when I decided I couldn't stand it anymore. I had to know.

Maybe it was all a dream. My argument with Tess and the pressure of the last few months could have created a hallucination. Stress hallucinations were a thing, weren't they? I couldn't help thinking about trying it again. I was drawn to it in spite of my every logical thought telling me to stay away. I wondered if I'd find it was basic, run of the mill weed all along, no magical effects. A small part of me wished that were the case, a part growing quieter by the second.

I snatched the bag from my desk and walked toward the elevator with the vigor of a speed walking mother of four. Seth called out as I crossed his desk but was too slow to catch me as the metal doors of the elevator closed. I met his eyes through the shrinking crack and tried to give him a short, apologetic shrug.

I paced around the enclosed space, keeping time with the melodic beeping of each floor. My mind was frantic with asinine questions. Would Tess notice the bag was gone from the trash? Would Seth rat me out to my wife? What was this stuff, anyway? What if it was poisoning me? What if my life was in danger—The questions stopped the moment the doors opened to the lobby.

It was him, the man from the elevator.

When his eyes met mine, they widened in surprise, his mouth pulling into a tight line. "Fuck," he whispered under his breath. In an instant he turned on heels and dashed out of the building, rivaling even my pace from moments ago.

I ran after him. "Hey! Wait! I need to talk to you," I called out.

I danced around a maze of people, blurting out half-formed, half intended apologies to the unsuspecting victims he had pushed through. I watched through the glass doors of the lobby as he reached the sidewalk and took off with a sprint. I gave nary a moment's thought before sprinting after him.

I pursued him across several city blocks, impressed by my own ability to keep track of his bobbing head through the sea of midday lunch goers. I had almost caught up to him when I was thrown to the ground with a sudden and unmistakable force.

A young kid wearing a hat that read 'Pizza Steve' stood above me. His face was contorted by horror and shock. He was spewing frantic words, but my pounding head could make no sense of them.

I had always thought it was a New York right-of-passage to get hit by a bicyclist, but the experience was far less satisfying than I thought I would be. I pushed myself off the ground, groaning through the aches screaming in my bruised joints and compelled my body to continue its chase of the mystery man. The delivery boy called out after me, but I paid no mind, I had far more important things to worry about.

I had lost sight of my mysterious benefactor during the accident, but hoped luck might win out as I turned left at the end of the block. He was standing alone in a tight alleyway, back leaned up against the wall, one leg bent and pressed against the brick. He was smoking a cigarette.

That bastard was waiting for me.

Despite my suspicions, I didn't hesitate on taking my chance for answers.

"Tell me who you are! What is this?" I shook the bag in his face, trying not to display the pain I was still in from that biker collision. It was evident my efforts were in vain because he chuckled, taking in another puff and not even glancing in my direction.

"Quite a tumble you took back there, pretty boy." The man smirked at me, unfazed by my manic state.

"I'm fine, no thanks to you. Now tell me what I want to know." I shoved his shoulders against the wall. There could be no opportunity for him to take off again. I couldn't handle another chase. He remained unbothered by the entire encounter. In fact, he appeared amused. He stretched his hand behind my arms to take yet another puff, blowing smoke right in my face.

"Easy there, mate. This here is precious goods." He gestured at the cigarette between his fingers. I finally realized that wasn't tobacco smoke I smelled. It wasn't weed either. This was a unique scent, something that, before last night, I had never smelled before.

Understanding softened my face, and I loosened my hold on his shoulders, taking a few steps back.

"You tried it, huh?" he said. "The name's Jamie. Let me buy you a drink and we can chat about the little taste you've had of this operation."

"Operation? You mean there's more?" I questioned.

"Let me buy you a drink. I'll explain everything." Jamie sauntered back toward the busy streets as he called after me, "This way, buttercup. I know a lovely little pub around the corner."

I had no choice but to follow him.

* * *

He was two pints of Guinness in and had said next to nothing for thirty minutes. I sat across from him, taking in everything I could. He had a gruff exterior with a scraggly, patchy beard taking hold of his upper lip and neck. His hair was thinning and combed back in a way that it covered most, but not all, of the balding spots. He wore a thick wool sweater that appeared to have been quite a nice piece at one time but had been worn and washed frail over too many years. It hung loose on him, a few sizes too big. His face was slightly gaunt, the dark circles under his eyes made more apparent by the hollowness of his cheeks. It was clear the man hadn't eaten consistently for quite some time.

"I work for a powerful person who's keen to turn this shit storm all around us into a profitable equation. You get what I'm saying?"

Now, in a calmer state of mind than before, I was able to register that Jamie had a thick Irish accent. His words struggled to push past his mustache and the near liter of beer he'd consumed.

"I can't tell you all the science behind it, but from what my employer has gathered, the color didn't up and vanish." He flourished his hands as if he had produced a puff of smoke in a magic show.

"We humans lost the ability to see it. Something messed with our neuron-receptor 'thingies.' It blocked our brains from processing color, but the mechanisms still work." He plucked the bag out of my clenched hands and shook it in the air, "That's where this stuff comes in. This is the new frontier."

I knew what he meant. When I had taken that hit, it didn't simply return the color to my sight; it created a whole new experience, full of otherworldly colors, textures and rhythms.

Jamie had barely finished his sentence before I blurted out mine, "I want in."

I didn't even know what 'in' meant, but I knew I needed a steady supply of this miracle cure to keep my business floating, to keep myself floating.

"It's not that simple," Jamie scoffed. "We already have a full list of clients, real high rollers too. We don't need some yuppie hogging the supply." He sat back with his arms folded across his chest.

"So, what," I asked, "you sell this stuff to your big A-list clients, and they get to re-experience the world in *techno-color*? It's some premium living kink?"

"Not all looks then, aye? You're getting it now. Unless you've got a fat wad of cash in your trousers, I reckon we are out of your budget."

He was right of course, I would have considered myself a successful man, but no one could compete against the money of New York high society. If I wanted in, I had to come up with some bargaining chips, and fast.

"What if I could sweeten the pot for you?"

Jamie took another gulp of his Guinness, raising a burly eyebrow as his only indication of intrigue.

I took that as my cue. "I own one of the most prominent art galleries in New York City. If you deal me in on this stuff, I can create and showcase an exclusive line of paintings for users. The material world is doing away with color. We already know it's happening. TV is going back to black and white, clothing designers are rethinking their collections, even flowers are going out of business. Sooner or later there's not going to be much worth seeing in color."

I realized I was sweating. I brushed my palms against my pant legs under the table, hoping Jamie wouldn't realize I was out of my depths here. "The only thing rich fucks desire is status. Luckily for you, sir, that is precisely my area of expertise."

It was a good business plan. I had spent all morning formulating what I would say to this man if I ever saw him again. As fate would have it, I hadn't had to wait long to give my pitch. The gallery was used to catering to a higher end clientele, that's where the money was. I knew these people inside and out. An exclusive line of paintings, made for users was the grand slam I needed.

"You make an interesting offer." He said nothing more while he swallowed the final swig of his pint.

I grasped my own beer firmly, watching the condensation droplets fall down the glass. Jamie hadn't asked when he ordered for both of us, and I wasn't about to complicate matters by bringing up my torrid past. If he noticed I hadn't touched mine, he didn't say anything.

He slowly rose from his seat, taking my confidence with him as he waddled toward the door. "Shit," I whispered dejectedly as I watched my dreams walk out the door in Jamie's brutish claws. Apparently, I wasn't the salesman I thought it was.

I watched him walk away, realizing he had taken my small sample bag with him. This ignited another round of swearing under my breath. I was working up the courage to go after him and demand he reconsider when he stopped a step short of the door. With a wave of his hand as he left, he tossed the small bag back at me.

I caught it midair as he called over his shoulder. "It's called Apollo by the way. Welcome to the space program."

11

East Village

You were hurting for longer than any person should.
You hid because you couldn't stand to be hurt again.

But then you met me, and you couldn't hide any more.

Disbelief. That's the only way I can describe it. Complete and utter disbelief. I gawked at the door, jaw agape. People don't do this! People don't make strange, vague deals with strange, vague men they met on an abandoned high-rise floor. And yet . . .

I rose from the table, smirking. I scanned the room expecting everyone to be grinning as widely as I was. Had they witnessed what had happened? Did they see the face of a man who had found an answer to his every problem? It was clear as I glanced around that the fantasy was in my head only. The other bar patrons glared at me out of principle as I strutted from the pub.

The wind was blowing through my hair, and I reveled in the glorious chaos. Each strand, once perfectly poised upon my head, was now thrown around in the blustery, sickly air of the city. Many days I had cursed the wind for its disruption of my routine, creating mess out of order. I would grunt and sigh at the sky as it fol-

70

lowed its natural whims, coming in collision with a disillusioned me thinking I had the right of way with nature. Today I opened my arms wide and let the sun bake into my sorry face. The air tickled the wisps around my ears and waved hello to my overcoat as it passed through, on its way to the next person. I sucked in the sweet smells of dog piss and trash day. Then I started walking.

My mind wandered alongside my feet and pondered the perplexities of life's coincidences. Life is a fickle fellow. Not dissimilar from a distantly related Aunt who pesters you at every family gathering. She pokes and prods into your life asking about career advancements and failed relationships. She picks at every insecurity until you leave as a shell of yourself. Your every sense screams that you should disregard her nagging for sake of your own sanity. Yet, for some strange reason you want nothing more than to win her approval. Nothing is ever good enough for your dear old Aunt. Come to think of it, life wasn't a fellow at all. No, life had to be a woman. A woman whom, despite her complexities and her standards, I loved. She was as kind and selfless as she was critical and demanding. This woman cares for strangers with the same intensity that she cares for family. Through her complexities, her morals run her life and provide firm ground for her to stand on. She is a dichotomy of actions, and she is both my salvation and my destruction. Yes, life was a woman indeed. And her name was Tess.

There was no turning back now. I knew I would have to tell her everything, eventually. I'd tell her about Jamie, about Apollo, about the new life I had signed on for. But if I had any chance at her understanding, much less accepting, my choices then we had groundwork to cover first. It was midday, and I should have been heading back to the studio for more depressing expense reports, but my feet found a familiar path instead. Tess and I met at the Sixteenth Street Recovery Clinic. I tried to avoid going back there often, it brought back too many memories, but these were special circumstances. I braced myself for the walk. It wasn't far from Soho to my old East Village haunts, but memory lane can be a costly detour. It hadn't even been five years since it all went down. When I think back on those times, it's as if the memories belong to a stranger. I was a different person then and that abhorrent stranger's actions were not mine. The truth of this scared me, more than I wanted to admit, which is why I shied away from remembering. I found myself on the corner of 10th St. and Avenue A when the past I desperately tried to forget came flooding back to me.

Long before I owned my own studio, I was lucky enough to secure a small showcase at a gallery in Washington Heights. A few pieces had made it into galleries before, selling for a couple hundred bucks or so, but this was the first time I'd tapped into the big leagues. A showcase all my own and almost half had sold on opening night. I walked out the door that night with a couple grand burning in my pocket. It was what every great artist dreamed of, or what I had dreamed of at least, and from there, the offers kept coming. I was commissioned for another showcase in a short two months' time.

I was young, stupid, newly wealthy and surrounded by bad influences in New York City. It didn't take a mind reader to know how that was going to end. I was barely sleeping trying to keep up with the demand for my work. My creativity was at the end of its rope, and I still felt like an imposter walking around in stolen shoes. That's when I met Marc.

Marc was the son of a big-wig financial advisor on Wall Street and grew up with Ben Franklins as bed fellows. Marc fell into the trap many rich city boys do and became resentful of everyone and everything, except, of course, drugs. Marc's father saw him as a failure and instead of paying for an Ivy League education Marc was shipped off to the penitentiary also known as Alabama for university. Little did Marc's father know that rednecks love to party just as much as prep school kids.

Flash forward six years and Marc is back in New York, still has a drug problem and still hates everything, especially his father. Except now he has a southern drawl when he drinks. That's when I met Marc, or more aptly I found him. Before I was an 'uptown-er,' I lived in a greasy basement apartment near Tompkins Square Park. I negotiated a cheap rent with the bar upstairs in exchange for taking out the trash and shooing away the drunks who passed out on the stoop. Before Brooklyn, East Village was the place for all trust fund kids to 'slum it' for a night and pretend to be less pretentious than they were. The irony was that they ended up partying with all the exact same assholes they went to school with, worked with and lived next to, except forty blocks south of home. Usually this was a pretty sweet gig because these kinds of drunks tended to hand me fistfuls of cash as I helped them into taxis. They didn't put up too much of a fight either, unlike the drunk teenagers who had stolen their older siblings' IDs for a night out. Those assholes got angry when you cut them off.

At first, Marc was one more the faceless rich kid I called a cab for. It was late, nearly sunrise, and I had barely slept in days while prepping for my next show. Maybe sleep deprivation was the motivating factor, but for some reason I took pity when he started crying. Crying wasn't unusual in these instances. I found that most people cried when they drank, but this was different. It wasn't a messy kind of cry that screamed for attention. Silent tears rolled down Marc's face. He sniffled into his hundred-dollar dress shirt.

"What if there is no light at the end of the tunnel?" he asked. His voice was soft but steady. "What if, when all is said and done, when we achieve all this greatness . . . . what if we still feel shitty?"

His question shocked me. Not because of the clarity with which we asked it, but because on the nights when I was at my lowest, I had wondered the same thing. I offered to let Marc stay at my place that night. I didn't have a couch, but I made him a spot on the floor out of an extra blanket and some pillows. When I woke a few hours later, the blanket had been folded and a note saying nothing more than *Thanks* was left in his place; also, a handful of cash. I was sure that was the last I'd ever see of him, but lo and behold a few nights later I found him passed out on the street again. We continued this odd dance for several nights before Marc ended up on my doorstep in broad daylight. It was one of the only times I ever saw him sober.

"Hey," he said. He had a radiant smile; one I was sure came in handy often in his life. He stepped inside my apartment without an invitation and peered around intently. "I know I've slept here multiple times now, but this is the first time I'm truly seeing it." He continued his tour of the single room, intently examining all fifteen items I owned. He stopped at the stack of canvases in the corner and flipped through them.

"Please be careful," I stammered out. I was strung out on caffeine and slightly delirious by the thought that this goon might ruin one of the pieces I had stayed up all night finishing.

"I know what I'm doing." He chuckled, not even glancing back at me. "How much are you getting per show?" he asked.

I was confused by his question but for some reason decided to trust the near stranger pawing my work. "I usually get 40 percent of the sales, but I have to pay my own transport costs. It's a shit deal but it's all I've got right now."

"Hmm," was all he replied. He departed from the paintings and sat on the bed, flopping backward to stare at the ceiling, his hands folded across his stomach. He lay there motionless for several moments as my confusion quickly grew into annoyance.

"Look man, I know I've let you stay here a few nights, but that doesn't give you the right to come barging in. We're not exactly friends. I don't even know your name!" My voice quivered at the line between demanding and frightened, but Marc didn't appear the slightest bit bothered by it.

He sat up slowly, walked toward me, and extended his hand. "Marcus Alan," he said.

I shook his hand tentatively. "Killian St. James," I replied.

"Great!" he replied, "Now we're friends and you can call me Marc."

He flashed that smile again as he sat back down on the bed and assumed his lackadaisical position. This time though, he spoke. "Listen, Killian, I think you've got some real talent here and I appreciate you taking me in all those times. I've got some friends in the art game and I'm going to make some calls for you. You're right, 40 percent is a shit deal. I can get you 65 percent, plus a base salary of $5,000 per show, regardless of sales. You're gonna be big, trust me. I know a good investment when I see one."

The rest was history. Turns out Marc did have some prominent art world connections. Before I knew it, I had enough steady income to move out of the basement and into an actual one-bedroom. I was still living in the East Village, but now I had an elevator in my building and a door between the kitchen and the bedroom. Marc still crashed at my place almost every time he went out, which was every Friday through Sunday. I joined him once I had some free time. With better showcase deals, I didn't need to work around the clock, and truth be told, he was the closest thing

I had to a friend in the city. I can attribute much of my early success to Marc. His connections allowed me to bypass a decade of paid dues in a who-you-know game. At the time I thought all my dreams had come true but if I could go back, I'd shove his ass in a cab like all the rest. As much as Marc added to my life, he took far more.

Beneath his boyish charm and his carefree attitude, Marc was a controlling and manipulative person. Though I never met his father, I assumed the apple didn't fall far from the tree. He was a pusher, a 'have one more drink,' 'take one more hit' kind of friend. At the time I was too desperate for his help and too afraid of creative stagnation to turn down his advances. It didn't take long for me to join him as one of the drunks on the street.

I thought I had it under control. I suppose that's what everyone thinks. It was innocent enough at first, partying with Marc every night and making a killing at the galleries during the day. But eventually, one more hit wasn't enough for me. Marc gave me a direct line to his dealer so I could pick up 'supplies' anytime I wanted. That was the beginning of the end.

Before then, I had only been mooching off Marc's nightly stash. Having the limited access had fooled me into thinking I could control myself, turns out I was wrong. For the first time I realized how expensive drugs were. Of course, Marc only bought the good stuff, but even with the success I was currently having, I was too frugal to pay his prices. I ended up finding a dealer of my own who sold out of Tompkins. Marc's dealer might have been expensive, but at least his stock was pure. I found out too late that my guy was mixing his stock. Marc stuck primarily to weed and cocaine—the rich boy essentials—but I was unknowingly doing nightly lines of fentanyl. Things spiraled out of control quickly from there.

On the night that changed my life, I had made a killing at some gallery in Midtown. I truly couldn't tell you which it was, but I walked out with nearly ten grand. In addition, I signed a contract with the gallery owner for five more shows within the next six months. Marc said we should celebrate. That's the last thing I remember clearly.

There were models and whiskey and too many things that weren't made to be snorted. The one thing I do remember from that night is the high. I was at the top of my game, everywhere I looked I saw bright lights and beautiful women. This is what life was supposed to be all about. I checked all the boxes and there was nothing more to be done. Except, apparently, another line. Turns out what my doped-up brain thought was the bathroom counter tops was, in reality, the hood of a police car. I can attribute much of my early success to Marc, but I can attribute my addiction to him too.

Marc's daddy bribed the judge to let him off with a fine and a warning, but his benevolence didn't extend as far as his nobody artist friend. I was given the option of prison or rehab. It was an easy choice and saved my life in more ways than one.

Hers was the face that guided me through the detox. My ears were ringing, my eyes blurry and my head was pounding like a landlord demanding his three-weeks-past-due rent. My body was racked with sweltering chills for weeks, leaving me sore and exhausted. I wanted to sleep but was kept awake by the fire of desire burning me alive. The pain was blinding but through all the chaos I could see her face crystal clear. Her smile whispered sweetly to me. Her eyes filled with me with compassion. Fiery red hair cascaded around her face, illuminating her in a scarlet glow.

Once the initial detox was through, I was levelheaded enough to get to know the person behind the caretaker. We'd talk for hours a day during our therapy sessions. Her father was an alcoholic and had died of his sickness when she was a teenager. While she had conflicting emotions toward her father, she held no such quandaries for addiction and those afflicted by it. She was hired at the clinic the day she turned eighteen and never looked back.

I was immediately taken by her. Not only by an overwhelming sense of debt to her, but I was enamored with her drive to help others. She took her shitty situation and turned it into something positive. She was an inspiration. I spent six months in rehab and nearly every day I asked her to go out with me. She declined, of course, being the ethical counselor she was. Undeterred, I kept asking, turning it into more of a habit than a real request toward the end. I had given up hope she would ever accept, but it was a dream to focus on during my recovery. I kept at it all the way to the end.

The day I was released Marc showed up at the clinic. It was the first and only time he ever visited me. He offered a wordless apology in the form of a fresh gallery deal and a "quiet night out" to celebrate my sobriety. His bloodshot eyes and visibly thinning hair told the story of what he had been up to while I was in rehab. I knew if I accepted his offer, I'd end up right back there in no time at all. I graciously told him to fuck off and that I never wanted to see him again. For his part, he listened.

That same day Tess finally agreed to my request, citing I was no longer a patient, and it was no longer an ethical quandary for her to accept my advancements. I took her acceptance as a sign from the universe that I'd chosen the right path. I've never been one to believe in all that cosmic hocus pocus, but when a good thing happens, who am I to fight it?

The capacity for human kindness will never cease to astound me. There is so much going wrong in the world, it's easy to forget that there is a lot going right too. Tess is a constant reminder of this. She saved me back then. She brought me back to the land of the living. I will be indebted to her until the day I die. There's a constant guilt that we didn't meet under better circumstances. Each time I told her this she would smile and simply say, "We met the way we were supposed to meet Killian. I'm glad we did, no matter the paths we took to get there."

That guilt weighs heavier as I stared up at the very center where my life began anew. The center my Tess still worked at. Three years ago, I received a new lease on life there. Now I returned as a liar. I steadied myself and pushed through the foreboding metal doors.

"Killian! We haven't seen you around here much lately. Are you looking for Tess?"

"It's nice to see you, Kiara. Yes, I am, but it's supposed to be a surprise . . . " I trailed off, hoping she would pick up on my implied secretiveness.

She responded with a short gasp cut off with a tight-lipped smile. She held a finger to her lips and winked as she radioed for Tess to come to the front desk. Kiara was always animated. She had a pure heart and she had been a loyal friend to Tess for years. Seeing her again filled me with warmth.

"She'll be right here, hun. I've got to make some copies real fast. Are you okay waiting here until she comes down?" Kiara was already shuffling a large stack of papers and file folders into her arms before hearing my agreement.

I settled in with my elbow leaning on the desk, peeking at one of the front classrooms while I waited. The center showcased the enrichment classrooms near the front desk so visiting families would get the impression that everyone here was having the time of their lives. The giant glass windows revealed walls lined with messy paintings and shelves filled with clumsy clay sculptures. I surprised myself to find I was smiling as I remembered my own experiences in that same room. I had understandably been a frequent flier in the painting groups during my time here.

My eye caught a woman in the back corner, slumped in her seat. A paintbrush twitched in her hand while she stared blankly at the canvas in front of her. I couldn't see what she painted, but from her face, she wasn't happy with it. The instructor came over to the woman with a painfully compassionate smile spread across her cheeks. I couldn't hear their discussion behind the glass, but the woman never moved her blank stare from the canvas.

In a split second, the catatonic woman lunged. Paintbrushes went flying and canvas was knocked to the ground. The woman was blindly throwing paints and dirty water until several orderlies rushed into the room to remove her. It was a sad reality that this wasn't the first outburst I'd seen during art class. I knew all too well that recovery was not always smooth sailing.

The rest of the participants, the instructor included, quickly returned to normal, unfazed by the sudden outburst. Yet, even from behind the glass I was unexpectedly startled by the experience. A lump formed in my throat as my pulse throbbed. A pounding in my ears threatened to take over all my senses. I tried to keep the fear at bay as I pictured myself in that art room, throwing a tantrum and losing my mind from withdrawal. I was startled out of the mirage by a soft hand on my shoulder.

"Killian? What are you doing here?"

There she was, angelic as ever. She wore dark scrubs, and her hair was tossed together in something resembling a bun, held together by a large claw clip in the back. I pulled her close to me, savoring the smell of her shampoo and relishing this small moment. My heart steadied itself and my breath returned to normal. She always saved me.

"Seriously, Kel, what's up?" She pulled away to look me dead in the eye. She had that tone that said she was in full interrogation mode. She'd never taken lightly to spontaneity.

"I am in a particularly good mood today and I wanted to see you. Can I take you out for dinner?" I flashed my best smile, the one I was hoping could hide my new secrets.

She lowered her eyes and gave me one of her classic stare downs. I could sense her trying to find an ulterior motive, but I held strong with my debonair smile.

"Okay. Yes, that sounds nice," she finally gave in. "I need to finish up a few things here but then we can go. Also, I'm picking." She turned with a smirk and strutted down the hallway.

"I'll meet you out front," I called. She replied with a thumbs up in the air, not stopping to turn back.

I quickly walked back through the metal doors, my eyes trailing the floor, careful to avoid the art room.

12

Fairytales

I used to believe that the terrible things I heard in the news were stories that happened in a world apart from my own. But the stories found their way in and I have become one of them. I now know that the world is as dark and cruel as I had hoped it wasn't.

"Seth," I hissed through my cracked office door. "Seth!"

Seth was wearing headphones and nodding his head along to an inaudible beat. His feet were propped up at his desk as he flipped through the pages of an art history textbook, seventeenth century Italian sculpture from what I could see.

I crumpled a piece of paper and lobbed it at him. I marveled at my aim as the little ball of paper plopped on his head. He startled and swiveled to face me, shouting over the volume of his music, "Did you throw a ball of paper at me?"

"Yes, now get over here." I motioned through the crack.

Seth squinted his eyes in confusion and made a show of over-dramatic offense as he sauntered toward my door. He took out his headphones and spoke at a normal volume. "You've been acting weird the past few days. What is going on?"

It had been three days since Jamie left the bar with his inventively vague instructions and I was going out of my mind, not knowing what was next. I needed to talk to someone and figure out how to proceed. Normally I would have talked through this sort of thing with my wife, but that was not an option in this situation. Seth was a man I knew I could trust.

I pointed toward the box sitting on my desk.

Seth approached and read the label aloud, "Addressed to Killian St. James of the Prince St. Gallery. No return address. Should I be seeing something here?"

"Seth, have you ever heard of something called Apollo?"

"I'm assuming you don't mean the rockets," Seth replied hesitantly.

"No," I chuckled. "Seth, I met someone—"

"Sir, does your wife know?"

"What? No, not a woman." I huffed and sat in my desk chair, motioning for Seth to take a seat. He stared at me, wide eyed and brow furrowed.

"Let me start over. Seth, what if I told you that we could see color again, and not just the way it was? A whole new world of colors. Ones that move in front of your eyes and dance to their own rhythms. Colors you can't even imagine seeing. I know it sounds fantastical and impossible, but I've seen it, Seth. I've seen it with my own eyes."

Seth stared back at me blankly. It was as if the kid had short-circuited and the wires inside his mind were frantically trying to put themselves back together again. He stood from his chair and began pacing the room with a huff. He mumbled furiously in a silent argument with himself. He threw a hand to his head, scratching along his hairline. He let out one long, exasperated sigh before settling back into his chair. He leaned forward, his elbows resting on his knees. His hands were held in a prayer, with the bridge of his nose resting on the tips of his fingers.

"I'm listening," he said solemnly, not giving away any inkling of the thoughts behind his words. Watching his perfected, emotionless expression made me wonder if Seth was part of an amateur poker league.

I let out a steady sigh and told him everything. I told him about meeting Jamie in the elevator, about finding him on the street and the deal we struck. I told him about Apollo and what it showed me. It was such a sweet relief to tell someone all of this. I hadn't realized how much I was holding inside. Seth followed each detail of the story intently. He nodded here and there, but didn't say anything until I had finished my outlandish tale.

He spoke quietly, maintaining his blank expression, "Are you fucking with me, boss?"

"Seth, I am absolutely—"

"Because don't you *dare* say these things if they aren't true. I know this has been hard for you, but you're not the only one who lost something in the Fall." He stared at me with ice in his eyes. I had never seen this side of Seth. He was usually quiet and reserved. I hadn't witnessed him so much as raise his voice, much less the intimidating stare down he displayed. I was suddenly glad that he was playing on my team.

"This is not a joke, Seth."

He contemplated my words, closing his eyes and no doubt mulling over each possible scenario, one of which, I was sure, included calling an asylum.

Finally, he asked, "Is that what's in the box?"

"You believe me?"

"Jury's still out on that one, but if you are telling the truth, then the proof is in the pudding. At least that's what they say, I think." He gestured toward the box.

"Ah, yes, I suppose you're right," I replied. I was concerned over the ease with which he accepted what I laid before him but decided to play it out. I reached inside the top drawer of my desk for my pocketknife. "The honor's all yours, kid."

Seth sliced into the box and pried opened its flaps. Inside were several small bottles, which might have been prescription bottles with no label, meticulously packed in dark foam molding. A surprising amount of care went into packing this box, considering who I knew the sender to be. Jamie hadn't struck me as a 'handle with care' type of man, but I was glad to be pleasantly mistaken.

Seth slid one of the vials from its placeholder and smiled back with big, wanting eyes. He reminded me of a younger version of myself, especially when he smiled. A voice in the back of my head told me that it was now I who was playing piper. I was luring this unsuspecting child into a world I wished I'd never visited. I knew it was true, even if I wished it wasn't, but the play was in motion, and it was too late to stop it now.

"Is this stuff safe?"

The same thought had been buried in my own mind ever since I tried Apollo for the first time. I truthfully didn't know, but the reward it brought had to outweigh any potential risk. Didn't it?

"Nothing in this world is safe when taken in excess. Water can be as deadly as it is lifesaving," I mused, trying to satiate my own fears with this reasoning.

Seth nodded in satisfaction. "Are we going to try this shit out?" Seth toyed with one of the canisters, turning it about in his hand.

The boy in front of me smirked with the confidence of a child who didn't fully realize the consequences of his actions. I envied his boldness and longed for the days when I had that same youthful confidence. I wanted to turn back the clock to a time when I wouldn't have this pit in my stomach from what I was about to do. The funny thing about clocks is that they are always ticking. They march in an infinite cycle, no matter how hard you wish they might stop. It's only when it's too late that you realize they were marching toward a countdown all along.

"If we do this, Seth, there's no going back. You understand that, right? This isn't stuff you can hit once and forget about."

"I appreciate the concern, Boss, but I need this as much as you do." His cheeky smile was gone, replaced with a melancholy stare that said more than his words ever could. I wasn't the only one who was mourning.

"All right then. Go grab the paints and spare canvases from the storage closet. I'll meet you out there. If we're going to do this, we're going to do it right."

* * *

We were lying on the floor of the studio, both of us covered in paint. Surrounding us was a foreboding army of canvases of varying sizes. Neither of us had experienced truly liberated inspiration in a long a time. Even before the Fall, creativity was a difficult thing to find. Any professional artist knew that writer's block wasn't exclusive to words, but with Apollo, everything changed. With each hit, I was rediscovering the world. It was a unique exhilaration. Better than sex, but left me euphorically exhausted all the same.

"Best. Job. Ever." Seth chuckled, propped against the wall a few feet away from me.

I couldn't help myself from laughing in unison, but tried, in vain, to keep a straight face. "This isn't all fun and games, Seth. Nothing comes without a price."

"Whatever it is I'll pay it!" He called out into the empty room, flinging his arms open wide. He spoke like a drunken fool, but he made a fair point. I had been so distracted by the sheer presence of the box; I hadn't investigated its contents further than the canisters.

I struggled to push myself off the floor, my head spinning as I stood. I guess I felt a little drunk too. My vision blurred slowly into clarity as I stumbled toward my office. Right on top of the box lay a small white note card. When we had first rifled through the contents of the box, it appeared blank, but with Apollo in my blood, I could make out a faint line of writing. It was written in such a low contrast color that without the drug, it would be nearly impossible to see. I was impressed by the complexity of this operation. It hinted at larger players in this game than our friendly neighborhood drug dealer, Jamie. I made a mental note to think about this further once I was more levelheaded.

I stumbled back toward the studio to read it aloud with Seth. As I opened it up, a second note slipped out and fell to the ground, skittering across the concrete to where Seth was sitting.

"The deal is two ounces to start and then refills when needed. As I'm sure you're aware, a little goes a long way. Jamie," I read. Isn't that the fucking truth, I thought.

"What do you have over there, Seth?"

"I think it's a guest list," he replied. "It's got a bunch of names on it and a date . . . next Friday, I think. Does this Jamie guy want us to have a party?"

I was certain that was precisely what Jamie wanted. "I guess it's showtime."

Seth let out whoop and punched his hands in the air. I was going to need to buy that kid several espressos before sending him home. The effects of Apollo were already wearing off, but the haze and the fog remained painfully apparent, far longer than the last time. I rubbed my eyes, trying to force my vision to clear.

The fear that I was in too deep compounded in my gut, but the thrill of hosting a showcase again made my heart race. I looked around the studio, taking in the chaos Seth and I had created. This was the best work I had painted in years, Seth's too. Whether this was the right path or not, it was the one we had chosen. I had a studio full of paintings telling me to keep going, no matter the cost.

13

Interlude: Part 2

Few things came as easily and with as much clarity to Marc as this did: His encounter with the Empress was no dream. He slid open the door on his liquor cabinet, a sensation he was acutely familiar with, and selected a scotch from the back shelf. He poured himself a measure and then poured another. Swirling the liquid in his glass, he contemplated the encounter. He had spent days trying to piece together what happened that night. There were many questions to be answered, each answer leading to another equally intriguing question. He watched the liquid swirl.

It was his habitual reaction that poured the glass, but it was his newfound mystery that kept him from taking a sip. He needed his mind to be clear. For the first time in a long time, Marc had something to think about besides his own misery. It was time to take a walk.

He walked out from the subway station, temporarily blinded by the lights of several pubs sparking to life for the night. There was that familiar pull to enter their doors, but he resisted. He let memory guide him but was unaware of where he would end up until he hearkened upon his destination. He observed the modest building, straining his eyes toward the fifth floor. He knew full well that he wouldn't be able to see him from street level, but it didn't stop him from trying, anyway.

Marc had kept tabs on Killian after coming out of rehab, though never dared to make contact. He knew Killian would not take kindly to his presence, but he couldn't stop himself from protecting his friend either. Even if it was from a distance. They hadn't spoken in years, but Killian remained his closest, and arguably only friend; nothing would change that.

He stared at the glass lobby door from his shadowy position across the street. He tried to muster the courage to approach, now wishing he had, in fact, drunk that double of scotch back home.

He shifted from foot to foot, hoping the momentum would propel him across the street. His palms turned clammy, and a single bead of sweat ran down his neck. He took a deep breath and stuck one foot over the threshold of his side of the sidewalk.

His foot didn't have a chance to meet the pavement before he saw the elevator doors in the lobby open wide, with none other than Killian St. James appearing from within. All his progress reversed as Marc fled deeper into the shadows. His friend exited the building, deftly jogging around the block and disappearing into the mouth of a subway station. He sighed both from relief and disappointment.

This was not the first time Marc had found himself outside Killian's studio, though it was the first time he was sober. He noted the small victory before taking quick stock of his surroundings and plotting a course to the nearest bar. He would drink to both victory and defeat tonight.

He was about to step away from his curb when he saw her. She was unmistakable, even in the dim shadows. She emerged from the darkness deftly, her slender build appearing to glide out of thin air. She was illuminated by the overhead streetlamp, momentarily encased in a brilliant aura of light. She watched Killian disappear into the darkness before turning toward his building. Marc was too far away to see her face clearly. Still, he could have sworn that he saw a glint of a smile flash under the streetlamp before the Empress tucked her head and walked into the lobby.

Marc's heart sped up as he watched her standing before the elevator, glancing anxiously back and forth as she waited. Eventually its giant claws opened, and she disappeared within.

Marc was unsure of what he witnessed, but knew it wasn't good. More answers and more questions filled his mind. A common occurrence, he was finding, when the Empress was involved. He didn't know what she wanted with Killian, but he knew that her presence was no coincidence.

Marc had made many mistakes in his life, some of which haunted him to this day. He let his friend be ruined by sin once before and it cost him their relationship. This time, he feared it would cost Killian much more than that. He could not let history repeat itself, not for his own sake, but for Killian's.

This time, he would do the right thing. He would protect his friend now like he hadn't done before. He knew he wouldn't be able to rewrite history, and he had his doubts about changing the present, but he made a silent vow on that darkened street corner. A vow to do everything in his power to ensure Killian's future.

It was time to get the band back together.

14

Wildfire

I knew it all. I knew it all along. And I still stayed with you.
I stayed with you for too long.

I begged Tess to accompany me to the opening night of the showcase. I didn't have to beg hard; she would have come whether I asked her to or not, but I wanted her to know how much I valued her presence there. For the first time in a long time, I was reminded of my need for her. I had forgotten the serenity her partnership brought. Even before the Fall I had been pulling away from her. I was lured by a false notion of success. I thought I would only achieve my dreams if I achieved them alone.

What a foolish mindset that was. I've always heard that 'it takes a village,' but only recently did I come to truly believe it. Still, knowing something and doing it are two different things. I would lay in bed at night and waves of indecision, guilt and shame slammed into me with hurricane strength winds. In those moments, it's difficult to remember to breathe, much less to ask for help. Besides that, those were my problems to face, not hers. It was unfair of me to ask Tess to jump into my murky waters too. I was such a fool.

That night was different. It was more than a gesture of good faith to have her with me. I needed her to *like it*. Her opinion meant more to me than anything a critic or blogger could say ever write. To know I had her on my side would push back the fears and doubts swirling in my gut.

This was far from the first time I had shown my work to the public, but I was out of practice. I was plagued with a nervousness in my bones that I had become unaccustomed to. A few months ago, I was certain this chapter of my life had ended. That I would never experience the awe of seeing my work on display for the first time again. I had resigned myself to that. As the gallery had grown, I became more of a facilitator and less of the main attraction. Things were different now. The stakes were higher. The Fall changed everything.

Many believed that everything would simply fall into place, that society would return to its previous state. I knew this was a lie. Nothing would ever be the same again. That's why this *had* to work.

We trudged up the Prince St. stairs to meet a throng of mindless drones. Soho was bustling during the day, filled with wannabe influencers and rich-kid socialites who spent their days brunching instead of working. At night, it was amplified. Each neighborhood of the city catered to a specific taste. Soho is where people greeted the night, clocking out from their jobs and heading straight to happy hours. After a round or two of drinks, the crowds would unanimously dissipate to the second destination of the night—maybe East Village, Greenwich or Williamsburg (for the particularly adventurous). This neighborhood was never the destination of the night, only a pit-stop along the way, and for that I would always be thankful. I trudged through selfie sticks and practiced poses, my mission in control of my mind. I held Tess's hand tightly, leading her through the masses to stay close to my side.

"Killian, what's with the rush? We're nearly forty-five minutes early for the show," she called from behind.

"I want to make sure everything is perfect. You know, it's been a while since I've shown my work on a stage. Everything needs to go exactly according to plan," I said.

She replied with a squeeze of my hand.

We reached the door to the building, paused for a moment, and took a deep breath. Tess analyzed my movements. I saw her out of the corner of my eye, but didn't want to meet her gaze for fear of her questioning. I didn't want to let her know how truly terrified I was. For one, I had a nagging fear that she would see through my lies in an instant. That this whole adventure would be over before it began. But more importantly, I didn't want her to see how badly I needed this, how badly *we* needed this.

Ever since we met, I felt like the lost puppy she brought home from the pound, a project she kept around for fun. My gallery was the only thing that made me worthy of being with her. My art made up for all my other shortcomings. I needed that reassurance more than ever, to know that I brought something to her life that was as beautiful as what she brought to mine.

Tess softly turned my face toward hers. "There's more to the world than its colors, Killian. I know this isn't what you wanted it to be, but I'm proud of you for finding new ways to achieve the same result. It will get easier to adjust. I know it will."

Her words provided me with momentary comfort, as misinformed as they were. Still, they were enough to give me the strength to push through the door. The newest phase in the art world was geometric shapes and heavy textures. It was as close as you could come to interesting without color to ground the work. I had seen it on the art blogs I followed online. Other artists, struggling to find inspiration in a world where the rules had disappeared, posted their work, hoping for approval that wasn't coming. Trends were always changing. That was a fact that artists dealt with day in and day out. It was in the job description to stay relevant and adapt to the times, but this was more than anyone had bargained for. Art would survive in some capacity. Of this I had no doubt. But would those of us who shepherded it until now still be up to the task? The question still haunts me, but for the moment, I pushed everything aside to revel in the display.

The gallery was starkly blank. The floors and walls were painted white even before the Fall to emphasize the work, not the environment. Their harsh emptiness was ever more present now. I stopped to take it all in. I reviewed the parallel lines darting across the canvas and radiating rectangles highlighting the center point. Seth and I had both created pieces for the showcase, but I ended up with more floor space at his insistence. It was strange, seeing my art take on a new life. Had I not known the secret behind these works, I would be ashamed of giving into the trends of the times. This was not what I had imagined for my first showcase back, but I tried not to let the disappointment show too much.

I pulled Tess in close to me and wrapped an arm around her. "This is incredible, Killian," she said. She beamed up at me and smiled. "I think it's one of the best you've ever done."

She was being kind. We both knew this was far from my best work, at least in this light it was. Apollo would change my perspective, but I couldn't help the doubt clouding my mind and sinking into my stomach.

"Hey, Boss!" Seth came jogging over from a hidden corner of the gallery. "Pretty sweet setup, huh? Tonight is going to be epic! Oh hey, Mrs. St. James, it's good to see you."

"It's good to see you too, Seth." Tess chuckled and embraced Seth. "And we've been over this, please call me Tess." Surprise washed over Seth's face as he hesitantly hugged her back.

I laughed at the scene. Tess always had a way of breaking the tension. She wasn't bogged down by the semantics of arbitrary societal cues. She was a hugger and never shied away from her true nature. Her authenticity and warmth were contagious, like wildfire spreading through the room.

She broke away and gestured to the surrounding space. "You and my husband have been busy! Everything looks amazing here. I hope you're both very proud."

"Thanks Mrs.—ah, Tess. Thank you, Tess. That means a lot." Seth sheepishly grinned as we all stood around in awkward silence.

"I will take that as my cue. You boys go do whatever it is you do. I'm going to go see what you ordered for the bar. Hope you sprung for the good stuff, Kel. You and I both know Pellegrino is heads and tails above the rest." She wandered off toward the front, leaving Seth and me alone.

"All right, Seth, let's go find somewhere else to be before she figures out that I ordered store brand. My wife takes her sparkling water dead seriously."

* * *

"Little intimate, don't ya think, Boss?"

Seth and I stared at each other, practically nose to nose in the small bathroom of the gallery. It was moments before people would arrive, I hoped, and it was time for the finishing touches. "Yeah, yeah, I know. It's the only place here that has any ventilation, and we cannot risk you-know-who catching on to you-know-what we're doing here."

It was risky having her here in the first place. I prayed old habits would guide me through the secrecy and allow us to stay undetected by my wife's acute ability to sniff out suspicious behavior.

"Last chance to back out, kid." A part of me hoped Seth would take the out and spare himself from whatever chaos I had signed us up for; the other part was shamefully thankful to have someone in on the gag.

"No way. I've got as much at stake here. I'm with you, 100 percent." With that, Seth curled his lips around the joint and lit the end, sucking in deeply before coughing out a few moments later. I had to admit the kid was fearless.

I raised my own joint as if it was a glass of fine wine with which to cheer. "Bon voyage!" I said as I took in the sweet nectar of Apollo.

The effects were near instantaneous. I was Dorothy waking up in Oz. The world around me exploded into color. The gallery bathroom was as pale and stark as the rest of the gallery when empty. It wasn't much to see with or without color, but it was magic to watch the color flood back into my skin. I stared in wonder at my hands as the effects took hold. My eyes blurred and with each rapid blink came clarity and increased saturation. When my vision came back into focus, the color was back, too. I observed myself in the mirror. My skin was electric. I could practically see the blood flowing through my veins. It pulsed and flowed in microscopic rivers under the surface. It was as if the billions of tiny lights had come alive to welcome me into their world. I gripped the edges of the porcelain sink as my mind adjusted to the onslaught of sensation. I inhaled deeply, steadying myself.

That's when I saw it.

I hadn't noticed it the other times. I was far too concerned with the world around me to focus on my own appearance. Now, I was taken aback. Not only were my eyes seeing color again, but they had *become* color. My irises had turned the most violent shade of red, glowing like taillights. I should have been more concerned by this unexpected revelation, but the whole situation was strange enough that I brushed it off as yet another thing I couldn't explain.

"Ah, Jesus fucking Christ," Seth exclaimed loudly.

"Seth, what is it? What's wrong?" I gripped his shoulders, staring at him intently. His eyes were crimson, too.

Seth, oblivious to my discovery, continued in his exclamation, "I look like a damned fool! I thought I picked a cohesive outfit but look at me! I'm wearing *pink* pants, man,"

My heart rate instantly dropped along with my hands from his shoulders. I couldn't help but laugh. I laughed harder than was warranted, harder than I had in months. Seth attempted to maintain his frustration but was soon joining in my barrel laugh. Seth's outfit was ridiculous. His trousers were indeed pink, albeit more of dusty rose than Malibu Barbie. His shirt was a deep turquoise. The pairing was vivacious, but it could have been worse.

"Seth, why do you even own pink pants?" I inquired.

"They were part of a Halloween costume a few years ago," Seth replied, sounding deflated, "Man, I thought I was wearing navy and gray. Everyone will think I'm an amateur."

"It's not that bad," I lied. "Besides, the only people who will know are here for a show. You're just very on theme." I barely got out the last few words before breaking into a laugh again. "Anyway, if you think that's off-putting, check out your eyes."

Seth leaned in, opening his eyes wider with his fingers. "Talk about spooky." The glass fogged as he leaned close to examine the change in his reflection. "I guess it'll be easy to tell who else is on the same stuff we are."

For better or worse, there would be no hiding from the truth tonight.

* * *

"What are you drinking, darling? A G&T? Love that for you. Deliciously classic. I'm more of a vodka-cran bitch myself, but you know what? You've inspired me. I'm going to order one too. I haven't had gin since I was sixteen and raided my father's backup supply. It's fun to reminisce, isn't it? So provincial!" A man in the tightest pair of skinny jeans I had ever seen was walking away from Tess, chuckling to himself maniacally. His outfit was nothing too out of the ordinary—a T-shirt, a suit jacket and some loafers—but he reeked of expensive taste. He was a near copy of every rich socialite I saw every day. I could almost guarantee the ensemble cost upward of $2,000, the reason for which I couldn't begin to explain. As the man sauntered away, Tess turned on her heel, an uncomfortable smile plastered across her face. She caught my gaze and raised her eyebrows.

"Kel, the crowd at these events is always special, but the guest list tonight is something else. Where did you find these people?" she hissed.

She was right. This group did sway more toward the pretentious and out-of-touch than usual. Art galleries in Manhattan were always filled with fools who had more money than brains, but they could usually tell fine art from Target's home section. Tonight's crowd, courtesy of Jamie, was, I assumed, not rich art lovers but rich 'partiers,' far more concerned with getting high than reviewing the art. As the night continued, it became increasingly clear the role I was meant to play in this operation. It didn't matter what

I put on these gallery walls; I was now hosting the most exclusive speakeasy in town.

"They are. . . unique, honey, but it's difficult to find people who want to come to these sorts of things right now. You know how it is." It was the truth. I'd read that the Met was at almost a quarter of the attendance for the third week straight since it had reopened. No one wanted to be reminded of how the world changed and sadly, art was one of the biggest reminders there was. If even the Met wasn't immune, no wonder my own studio was struggling. Apollo was more than a gateway to the past; it was my only hope of keeping the doors open in the future.

"Yes, of course. I know times are hard, but seriously, Kel, . . . did you see that guy I was talking to? He was wearing hexagon sunglasses . . . inside . . . at night. The only people who wear sunglasses inside are—"

"Assholes and alcoholics," I chuckled in unison with her.

That was an inside joke we shared from our first days together. When Tess's father was in the worst of his addiction, he had amassed quite the collection of drugstore sunglasses to hide the fact he was constantly either hungover or drunk. He wore a pair everywhere they went, all the time. The day he died, she threw away every pair, citing she was neither an asshole nor an alcoholic, so she didn't need them anymore. To this day, she still refused to wear sunglasses at all. She went through summer days squinting and shielding her eyes, half blind out of principle alone. It was one of the things I loved about her. When she made a decision, she stuck with it no matter what.

"Another one is coming this way. You're on your own for this one. I'm going to go get a refill." She shook her glass to confirm her intentions.

I always made sure the bar was stocked with tonics of all sorts at these events. After her father, Tess swore off alcohol. I couldn't blame her, but sobriety is something that few people understand, and the questions were always too much for her. Years ago, she found that a glass of club soda with a lime slice was enough for everyone to assume she drank exclusively gin and tonics.

"Oh, remember, don't look them in the eyes. They'll suck out your soul with their lifeless babbling," she whispered before darting away.

If only she knew how on the nose she was. Every single person here, aside from Tess and the bartender, had the same blood-red eyes as Seth and me.

"Excuse me, sir. I want to inquire about purchasing a few of your pieces." The approaching voice startled me.

I turned and came face-to-face with another set of bleeding eyes, except these were familiar. He hadn't changed much since the last time I laid eyes on him, apart from his eye color, of course. He wore a suit that dripped with expense, as always, but I noticed his shoes were scuffed. Marc had always worn the shiniest dress shoes in New York. He rode exclusively in taxis and rideshares, never daring to brave the subway. Only the elite of the city could achieve shoes as flawless as his. Now that traffic had been all but halted from redesigned traffic signals, it appeared Marc finally crossed over into the real world, subway card and all.

"Marc. It's been a long time." I tried to hide the shock in my voice.

In truth, I was surprised I hadn't run into him sooner. New York City was a surprisingly small world, especially when you didn't want it to be. The fact that this was the first time I laid eyes on him in over three years proved he was avoiding me as much as

I was him. "I think I would have remembered seeing your name on the guest list."

"Oh, come on now, Killian, you know I have connections in the art world. Hell, I paved the road for this little studio of yours," he retorted with a huff.

"You may have gotten me some gigs, Marc, but you and I both know I clawed my way here, no thanks to you," I snarled back.

"I'm sorry you see it that way. Whether you want to admit it to yourself or not, I put you on the map."

I spat back, "Not to be rude, but what the fuck do you want, Marc?"

Marc's presence was not one I wanted to welcome. He was a threat to the delicate equilibrium I recently secured with my wife. She would not respond pleasantly to me entertaining the man responsible for my addiction—regardless of the role he played in my career rise.

He replied calmly, unfazed by my clear agitation, "This is a sweet little operation you've got here. A lucrative one I'd wager too. Don't think I haven't noticed the sales tonight. A word of warning to you, then I'll be gone. Be careful how far down the rabbit hole you go. The people you're dealing with won't think twice about cutting you out the second you've lost your value, or even worse, become a liability."

"What are you talking about, Marc? What do you know?" I demanded.

"All I'm saying is that you're racing against a ticking time bomb, old friend, in more ways than one. Be careful who and what you place your trust in. This is a new frontier we're living in, and the old rules won't apply for much longer."

It dawned on me what he meant. All of this would soon be phased out. Once their current supply ran out, distributors would stop selling pigments. All colored paints were already on a steep discount since the Fall. It was far cheaper to mix only black and white. All the Apollo in the world couldn't fix a world that had abandoned the past. Marc was right, I was fighting a timeline I hadn't even known existed.

He must have seen the realization in my eyes because he nodded and smiled an all-knowing smile. "Now you see it," he said, "I know there's some muddy water between us, but I still want the best for you. I came here tonight to warn you and now that I've done my moral duty, I'll walk out of your life once again."

Always a man of his word, Marc turned to leave, parting with one more sentiment over his shoulder before disappearing behind the elevator doors. "I'm assuming that gorgeous redhead over there is your wife. She's quite a catch, Killian, you're a lucky man. I'd watch over her if I were you. This room is full of vampires willing to do *anything* for the opportunity to worship pretty things again. Your wife might be the most beautiful piece on display tonight. I especially love those big brown eyes."

The elevator doors closed with a ding, filling my heart with terror as Marc descended below. Every person in the room suddenly became a threat. What was once a gallery full of simple rich jerks was now a war zone with predators lurking around every corner.

All this time I had been wrapped up in hiding the truth from Tess, trying to tell myself she would be better off if she didn't know the truth. Now I saw with piercing clarity that I was only protecting myself. I had practically gift wrapped her and sent her into a room full of beasts who knew in one glance that she was not in on their game. She had a target of *my* making on her back, and she didn't have the slightest clue.

The tables had turned, and I was faced with an impossible choice. I hated myself for even asking: Which was I willing to lose—Apollo or her?

15

⚜

Good Morning New York City

She wakes—afraid of what the world will bring her way.
Her heart beats in the shadows of her many scars.
It says, look to the sun. It shines bright like your soul.
But the scars cloud her heart until she can't see any sun at all.

The sun was blinding as I exited onto the humming street. The familiar, rank smell of city sidewalks filled my nostrils. Smell was one of those things you got used to while living in this city. Everything smelled. There were too many people and too many pissing dogs and too much garbage and not enough care to do anything about it. The smell followed you around, always the same no matter what borough you traveled to. Sometimes a reprieve in the form of cigarettes or marijuana would flood the nostrils. But mostly, it was just a *smell.*

God, grant me the serenity to accept the things I cannot change . . . The words played in my head as I tried to hold back the rage boiling inside me. They were wise words. It is foolish to be angry with

105

things you cannot change. But today that smell was going to put me over the edge.

"I know you weren't excited about getting glasses Kel, but I think they're pretty sexy if you ask me. It's very James Bond debonair." Tess was following me out of the store, oozing with desperation to cheer me up.

We had spent the last three hours walking back and forth along a wall of frames. I swear they were all the same. I hated every one of them, but it had become clear in the last several months that my eyesight was not what it used to be. I was squinting at street signs and holding my phone painfully close to my face. I had noticed it, of course, but wasn't planning to do anything with the information. I was convinced that denial would solve the problem shortly. I was too young to need glasses, wasn't I?

Aging was something I never thought too hard about until it was suddenly upon me. Fine wrinkles and spots of gray hair stared back at me in the mirror, infiltrating my reflection overnight. I had never thought about needing glasses until Tess commented on it. Her good nature wouldn't let it go. She pestered me to go to the doctor until finally I listened, whether out of exasperation or genuine persuasion I still don't know. Needless to say, the doctor confirmed her concerns and suddenly I was at the absolute worst place to be on a Monday morning in New York City.

She had insisted on coming with me to pick out frames. She even called off from work for the morning. I knew she meant it as support, but all the coddling drew even more attention to what I was painfully trying to avoid. Picking out glasses is as close to misery on earth as I can imagine. I didn't want to be there. I didn't want to admit that I needed help, even from something as simple as corrective lenses. Accepting the glasses was one step closer to accepting the fact that I was aging, becoming the old man no young person ever believes they'll become.

All these things were true and yet the biggest kicker of all, was that I could see fine. I could see perfectly crystal clear, in the way that truly mattered. When I was on Apollo everything was aligned, not a sight out of place. It was only when the effects wore off did my vision deteriorate. I didn't want to see this dreary, monochromatic world, anyway. I discovered, however, that the whole of New York disagreed with me. They were all trying to convince themselves it wasn't that bad. If they could only see more clearly, maybe they wouldn't notice everything that was gone. Suckers, the lot of them. I knew the truth.

But, for the love of Tess and for the purely semantic reasoning of not tripping on furniture anymore, I conceded. The frames I chose were simple, dark and square. Tess was right, they were reminiscent of James Bond. In all honesty, they were nice glasses, but out of principle for the matter, I hated them, the store and the whole experience. I tried to deny it, but in that moment, I even hated her.

"I don't have to be back at the clinic for another hour, want to go grab lunch?" Tess smiled, attempting to lighten the mood. Her optimism was admirable, but I was too deep in my frustration to let her win. Nothing was going to salvage the morning; I wouldn't let it.

"I'm not hungry. Maybe another time. I should get back to the studio, anyway."

Her smile dropped for a moment before she regained her composure. "No worries!" she replied chipper, "I'll see you at home for dinner?"

"Of course." I gave her a quick kiss on the forehead and squeezed her hand gently before slipping away toward lower Manhattan. I glanced over my shoulder as I left. She was standing still in the crowd as a school of people swam around her. She gave a slight wave before finally letting go of her forced smile. Her eyes dimmed as she watched me walk away. A pang ripped through my heart at the sight, lightening the anger weighing on me.

I felt guilty for abandoning her, for dismissing her efforts to cheer me up. I shouldn't have taken my pain out on her; but sometimes it's easier to revel in your own misery.

16

Puzzle Pieces

Have you ever been homesick for a place you've never met? I've had this incredible premonition of home without knowing where it is yet. I could almost reach out and touch it. But it's only a dream. A fantasy I hold in my heart for the days when reality is too much to bear. A refuge that saves me from the nightmares I see when I'm awake.

We had another Apollo show scheduled for the last Thursday in January, which meant the studio was in chaos. The arrangement with Jamie had been working seamlessly for a little over two months and we'd hosted nearly a dozen shows in that time. Each was filled with a new crowd of glowing red eyes. I didn't pay much attention to the faces, though I thought I recognized at least a few people at each show. The showings were becoming more frequent; we'd had two in the past week and were flying through inventory. Seth and I spent most of our days basking in Apollo, throwing paint around as if we were little kids again. It was hardly sustainable, but that was a problem I was planning to solve down the road.

I lit a joint the moment I walked into the studio, calling to Seth through the chaos.

"Seth? Where are you?" I peeked around the front corner, expecting to see him in the main gallery. His voice called out from the back near my office.

"I'm back here. There's uh . . . " He trailed off, leading me to believe he had gotten quite a head start without me. He might already be on his second dose of the day. I continued the short walk to the back until the presence of an unexpected figure startled me to a halt.

"There's, um, someone here to see you," Seth stated sheepishly.

A woman leaned against my desk. Her head was tossed back in laughter from something Seth had said, long blonde hair trailed down her back. At the sight of her, I quickly flicked off the lit end of my joint and tucked the remainder behind my ear.

She rose from her graceful lounge and strode toward me. As she stood, I could take her in fully. She was strikingly slender but still maintained subtle curves around her hips and breasts. She wore a white, long-sleeved dress that conformed perfectly to every inch of her. Her neckline trailed down dangerously low, but otherwise she appeared poised to take on a room of stockholders. She had an air of professionalism and perfection all around her. I tried not to linger in my gaze, but she was objectively gorgeous, and in the light of Apollo she truly glowed.

Her lips curled gently into a smile as she extended a manicured hand toward me.

"Please don't stop the fun on my account."

Her hand bypassed my own, outstretched for a handshake, and trailed up my cheekbone behind my ear. She plucked the joint from its resting place and gently brought it between her lips. She raised an eyebrow, silently asking for a light. That's I finally noticed what I had been too distracted to before. Her eyes burned crimson.

I obliged her request, and as I held the flame, I caught a glance of Seth behind her with a face of disbelief and awe. I narrowed my eyes at him, pleading to keep his cool. As beautiful as this woman was, I still didn't know why she was here. I sure as hell didn't want to give away our next move before knowing what game we were playing.

"So, miss . . . " I trailed off realizing I didn't know her name.

"Pietra Perrault," she replied, "and sincerest apologies for the unannounced arrival. If you'll permit me, I'll explain myself."

I gestured toward my office chairs, and she nodded with a smile, accepting my offer. As she settled into her chair, I pulled around a set of stools for Seth and me.

She took a long pull from my joint before speaking again. "You've been making quite the hullabaloo up here in the city, mister St. James. We've heard about you all the way out west. You see, I run a small, but affluent gallery on the Las Vegas strip: the Perrault Collective."

Recognition sliced through my mind. The Perrault Collective was one of the most prestigious art galleries in Vegas, it brought in an exclusive and lucrative crowd. I couldn't believe I didn't put it together the moment she revealed her identity.

"Ah, you have heard of me then"—She smirked, reading the expression on my face—"then you know the caliber work I'm after for my clients. Vegas has many wild and wonderful things mister St. James, but you'll find it's not exactly on the cutting edge." She held the joint up to the sky as if it were a trophy. "This little miracle has only just made its way across the desert. Now imagine my surprise when I catch word that not only has New York been running supply for months, but there's already an exclusive art dealer in the game. Truly a remarkable business play. I must applaud you."

My heart sped up, flushing my cheeks. I was both flattered and alarmed by the information she had provided. If rumors about my operation had already traveled as far as Vegas, then most certainly the whole of New York knew. There were two things I knew for certain in this city: if you had anything worth a dime, there was someone around every corner waiting to take it from you. If what Pietra said was true, competition was knocking at my door.

"Yes, I see you putting the pieces together now. It won't be long before you're not the only shop in town anymore. Then things will go right back to where they were, with you competing against the masses in a painfully crowded market." She paused, surveying the expressions on both mine and Seth's face. She waited for a moment longer than was natural, playing to her crowd.

"I want you to do a showcase in my gallery. My city has only recently caught on to your trend but doesn't mean there isn't a hungry market for your *special collections*. You were the first in this mister St. James, which means you have invaluable experience. My clients are willing to pay for the best, as am I." With that she crossed her arms and took another pull, indicating it was now my turn to respond.

Seth's eyes burred into my skull as I weighed my options. "Ms. Perrault—"

"Pietra, please."

"Pietra . . . I'm immensely flattered by your offer; however, I must decline. My home, my life and my work are here in New York and that is where I will remain."

To my surprise, Pietra only nodded gently, unbothered by my refusal. She didn't strike me as a woman who took refusals lightly, and this impression frightened me. Nevertheless, I wasn't willing to take on more risk until it was my last resort. She rose from her seat, extinguishing the now spent joint in the ashtray on my desk. She walked gracefully toward the door, taking her time, I suspected, to both leave an impression and allow time for me to reconsider.

As she passed by my seat, she leaned in close and whispered in my ear, "For when you change your mind."

She slid a small, stiff piece of paper into my front pocket. Her scent filled my head as her fingers lingered on my shoulder for longer than was warranted. A chill ran up my spine as the smell of pine and spice twirled along my collarbone. Then, as suddenly as she had overwhelmed me, she vanished. With her alluring presence gone from the room everything went cold and dim. I was left shaken and unnerved, my hands tapping an anxious rhythm at my sides. Pietra affected me in ways I couldn't explain, nor wanted to understand, spreading panic through my heart.

Seth let out a long huff of air and paced around the room. "I'm sure you have your reasons, boss, but I don't think I would have had the balls to say no to that lady."

"I almost didn't," I admitted, "but something isn't right about this whole thing." I racked my brain trying to pinpoint what that 'something' I referred to was. I couldn't put my finger on it, but our encounter with Pietra Perrault had been equal parts entrancing and threatening.

"I don't know what you're talking about, I felt nothing *but* right from her." Seth's face bloomed red as he tried to hold in his amusement, but we both quickly erupted in laughter. It was a welcome reprieve from the heightened emotions of the day. Seth had become a trusted partner through all of this, and it was comforting to have someone to confide in. I was grateful for his presence today and for whatever loomed beyond the horizon. One thing was crystal clear from our encounter: the stakes were higher than either of us had imagined.

Confusion crept in as I heard the elevator doors to the studio open once more. I sent a puzzled glance Seth's way, silently wondering if Pietra had come back for another round of negotiations. Seth shrugged his shoulders in equal perplexity. We both waited with bated breath, listening to heavy footsteps leave the elevator and stop short after a few feet. Silence hung heavy in the air until a voice called out from the front room.

"Hello?"

I knew that voice. It brought me back to five years ago, in that basement studio where I kept an extra blanket for that inevitable knock on my door. Marc was standing with his hands in his pockets, subtly rocking back and forth on his feet. He didn't notice me at first but made a bee line for my direction once he spotted me.

"Killian. I'm sorry for showing up unannounced, I'm sure you don't get many uninvited visitors here."

"More than you'd think," I returned dryly. "What are you doing here, Marc?"

"Right, of course. I'm—can we talk somewhere more private?" Marc narrowed his eyes at Seth who was standing in the doorway of my office.

Under normal circumstances I wouldn't have been the slightest bit inclined to give into Marc's request, but something about his presence was different. His eyes darted back and forth wildly, and his hands ran circles around each other in a nervous fidget. The anxious man before me was not the same one who I'd known all those years ago. I also had to admit that ever since his brief and mysterious appearance at the first Apollo show, curiosity had been gnawing away at me. I needed to know why he was back in my life and, more importantly, why now.

"Seth, I'm famished. Would you mind picking up lunch from our usual spot? This will only take a minute," I called over my shoulder, not daring to break eye contact with Marc. I was indulging him for now, but I wanted to let him know it was on my terms and my terms alone.

Seth silently walked past us into the elevator. His eyes weighed heavily on me as the doors slowly shut. He might have been worried, but I knew who I was dealing with. I'd been here before.

"All right, Marc, you got your privacy. Care to tell me why you're here?"

"I know you've been using Apollo to sell exclusive collections."

"Obviously. You were at the damn showcase! Is that all you came here to tell me?" I tried in vain to keep my voice from rising in frustration.

"No! No," he continued, "I came here to say that I have some information about Jamie. That's your dealer, right? Jamie is supplying more than you. He's dealing all over town. He's even selling to other artists."

"Jamie is a drug dealer, Marc. I didn't expect I was his only buyer. Regardless, I already know all this. Do you have anything useful to say or are you going to stand there and waste my time?" The truth was I didn't know all this. I had suspected as much, sure, but my conversation with Pietra had proven I had woefully underestimated the reach of this drug. I wasn't prepared to deal with insurgent competition. As much as I didn't want to admit it, if Marc knew more, then I needed to listen.

"There's something else. I know a few guys who got into this stuff early, real new wave stoners. Point is, they claim they've been smoking this shit since before the Fall."

"Before the Fall? What would be the point of that?"

"Killian, you know as well as I do that these people don't use logic as a reason for anything they do, but they claim the effects were even stronger before the Fall. Anyway, that's not the point. The point is that each of these guys have been smoking Apollo for almost a year and now every single one of them has gone blind."

My heart stopped.

"I see you're wearing glasses now, Killian. Have you been having vision problems?"

"Marc, stop this."

"Killian, it's already happening, isn't it?"

"Stop. No more."

"That's what I came here to tell you. I know we've had a rocky past, but I still care about you, Killian, and I know how much your art means to you. I couldn't live with myself if I knew this and didn't say anything." The sincerity in Marc's voice was alarming and added weight to the harrowing claims spewing from his mouth. "I couldn't live knowing I'd let you down again. Can't you see that?"

Fear boiled in me, turning the pistons of panic. My head throbbed and my heart pounded in a harmonious rhythm.

"I can see fine!" I had hardly realized I was yelling, but I couldn't stop. "In fact, I see everything *perfectly*! Five years ago, you came waltzing into my life and ruined everything. You turned me into a fucking addict, Marc. I've barely gotten my life back and now, when I find a solution to the *second* worst thing that ever happened to me, you try to ruin it all again. What is wrong with you Marc? Why are you obsessed with destroying my life?" I wanted to believe Marc's motives were pure, that he was trying to help, but our past was too murky, and his words were more anchors than lifelines.

"Killian, no, that's not what this is. You don't understand. I'm trying to help you!"

"Help me? By doing what? Scaring me off with ghost stories of 'mystery men' going blind? I bet one of your new asshole friends is trying to get in on this and you want me out of the picture so he can have all the spoils. I bet that's exactly what this is."

"There's no one else, I swear. I only want to protect you. This stuff is dangerous. I know I fucked up all those years ago, and it has haunted me ever since. I want to do things right this time."

They were the words I had wanted to hear for years, the apology that had never come. Yet, as I listened to his pleas, I felt nothing but betrayal, "That's terribly noble, but you're too late."

"Killian, I—"

"We're done here, Marc. I think it's best if you leave."

At that exact moment, the elevator doors dinged open to reveal Seth holding a droopy paper bag and two soda bottles. To his credit, Marc retreated to the elevator without another word. He sulked past Seth, his head hung low. I watched him with a burning glare until the elevator doors inched closed and I saw him mouth the words, *I'm sorry.*

"What was that all about?"

"Oh, nothing. A ghost from my past trying to stir up trouble."

I hoped that it was nothing. As despicable as his ruse would be, it was better than the alternative. If what he said was true, if Apollo was causing people to go blind . . . I stared sadly at Seth, holding a turkey bagel in his mouth as he twisted open his soda with both hands. The kid wasn't even out of school and now I had roped him into an impossible situation. If Marc spoke the truth, then both Seth and I were blind men walking. Worst of all, it was all my fault.

* * *

I was convinced that, of my two strange encounters from the day, both were spewing complete bullshit. But I wasn't certain. When I arrived home that night to find an empty apartment, I decided it was time to do some research of my own. I needed to put my mind at ease and reassure myself that Marc's words were nothing more than malicious fantasies.

I figured the best place to start was my friendly neighborhood drug dealer: Jamie, last name unknown. Jamie was the one tangible connection I had to Apollo's source and the only man I knew with more experience with it than me. If anyone could shine some light on the bigger picture, it was him.

Before my hunt commenced, I had to ensure that I wouldn't be caught by the one person who could sniff out suspicious behavior from a mile away. I set the scene with precision. I dimmed the lights in our bedroom until only the glow of the laptop screen illuminated me. I retrieved Tess's most expensive bottle of lotion from the bathroom and placed it within arm's reach of my side of the bed. I tossed my bedside tissues haphazardly onto the bed and stripped off my shirt, pants and underwear.

If Tess walked in while I was searching for Jamie, she wouldn't leave it alone. She'd pry for more information until I finally gave in, a result that was too dangerous to let happen. I couldn't endanger her with the knowledge I was hoping to learn. I had to get creative on how to distract her. All I needed was a plausible explanation as to why I was hiding away in our bedroom, suspiciously scrolling the internet. Sometimes the most complex problems have the simplest solutions. With the scene set as it was, I anticipated no further questions asked.

After an hour of scrolling through toxic internet forums, I found next to nothing. The only saving grace from this elaborate failure was the small piece of information I did manage to dig up: Jamie the drug dealer was legally James Moore. A name wasn't much to go on; it was barely better than nothing. I pushed my laptop to the side in frustration, eager to take a break from the endless dead ends.

As I was about to dive in for another round of fruitless efforts the bedroom door creaked open, and Tess walked in. I slammed the laptop shut and played my part as the horny husband, locking it in with a nervous grin that was only false in its origin. I watched her eyes survey the room and take in the scene I had laid for her, the pieces coming together before her eyes. I braced for impact but was greeted with a surprise instead.

The corner of her mouth turned up into a wry smile. Tess walked slowly to the bed, unbuttoning her white blouse with each step. She slowly crawled onto the bed, allowing me a stolen glance beneath her shirt.

We locked gazes with each other as she slowly bent down, meeting me face-to-face. Her eyes drew closer to mine as she whispered in my ear, "The next time you need a release, all you have to do is ask."

17

Written Correspondence

Write me as sculpture. Stoic, young and defined.
Write me as scripture. Lyrical, wise and unwavering.
Write me as song. Mysterious, whole and never-ending.
Write me as you see me, but whatever you do,
I beg of you, write me.

The room was a mess. Every pillow on the bed was no longer where it was meant to be. The sheets lay haphazardly strewn down one side of the bed. Tess had pulled up one section of the comforter to cover her lower half, much to my chagrin. I traced circles across her bare back as she lay on the bed next to me, a smile across her face.

"I told you those glasses were sexy," she murmured. Her eyes were closed from both exhaustion and comfort. She was a vision. I soaked her in and reminisced on the first time I saw her. She hadn't changed in all that time, even now in black and white.

"Penny for your thoughts?"

I smiled, back in the present. "I was thinking about the day we met. Do you remember that?"

She turned to face me directly, pulling the sheet up to meet her chin. "Remember meeting you? How could I forget? You were a complete and utter ass." She stuck the landing of her insult with a smirk but softened the blow with a gentle caress of my cheek. Her thumb traced my chin and pulled me closer for a kiss. Her lips turned up into a smile while pressed to mine. When we pulled away, her eyes glistened in the low light.

I might have been offended by her crass recollection of our first encounter if she wasn't absolutely right. I was an ass, and she had never let me live it down. One of the things I loved most about Tess was that she never took anything too seriously. Even my torrid past could be a source of amusement for her. She was the levity my life desperately needed.

I was ashamed that I had ever forgotten how much I truly needed her over the last year. Maybe if I had cherished her more, I wouldn't be in the mess I was in now.

"I am going to go wash up." She tapped my nose with a smile, quickly replacing her finger with a kiss. "Will you go see who's at the door?"

"What?"

"The door, darling, someone was knocking at the door. Didn't you hear?" She rose from the bed, pulling the top sheet with her and draping it around her body like something out of an old Hollywood movie. I wished I could spend eternity witnessing her, but the tilt of her head and the shoo of her hand reminded me that there was a mystery awaiting my attention.

I searched for the nearest article of clothing and quickly pulled on the pair of underwear I had purposefully discarded hours ago. I peered through the peephole of the door to catch the back of a man's head walking away from the door. I unlocked the deadbolt and stuck my head into the hallway. By then, the stranger was gone.

I shrugged and about chalked up the experience to a mistaken encounter when I noticed a small envelope laying on our doormat. There was nothing inherently menacing about the envelope itself. Nothing was even written on the front, and yet the sight of it made my hair stand on edge.

I swiped the note from its forlorn resting place and forced my trembling hands to pry its lips apart. The task was made more unsettling when compared to the typical transaction of modern-day communication. Words etched into paper are more permanent than words on a screen, and frightfully more dangerous.

Inside, a simple piece of paper lay in wait. On it was written two sentences. The card sat heavy in my hand, though it weighed no more than the average card stock. I read the contents tepidly.

Your actions have consequences. Are you prepared to pay the price?

All at once the apartment felt unsafe. I'd been powerfully violated by a mysterious entity. How could they have known that I was investigating Jamie a mere two hours ago? How did they know where I live? What else did they know?

With the snap of a finger, everything and everyone was now a threat. I gawked at the walls of my life. Originally, these were the walls of a blissful, carefree marriage. Then they became a cage for two people struggling under the restraints of circumstance. Now they were simply a prison, keeping me locked away until the moment of attack.

My mind was fixated on the image of whoever had delivered this harrowing message. I pictured him sneaking into the building, innocuously slipping past the doorman. He carefully padded up the stairs, making no notice of his arrival. He walked down my hallway, scanning the doors for my number. His hands had touched the same door I use every single day. His musk lingered in the stale air of the building. The thought of this stranger stalking my home was more terrifying than any ghost story I had heard.

Ghost stories elicit fear of the unknown. As a child, everything was unknown, making the supposed presence of the supernatural an unwelcome addition to the list of fears. As an adult, I knew there were far worse things to be afraid of. I knew these monsters are not only real but live among us.

"Honey, who was it?" Tess stood in the doorway to our bedroom, cloaked in warm shadows. She smiled her beautiful, innocent smile and all the trouble of the world faded away. I crushed the note crumple in my grip. Whoever *they* were, they sorely underestimated what it would take to scare me off. I dropped the shriveled piece of paper into the trash and returned my wife's smile.

"It was no one. The wrong address. What do you say? Should we call it a night?" I strode to meet her across the room and stroked her cheek with the back of my hand. Her own hand rose to meet mine as she leaned in for a kiss. Her lips were the soft flicker of a candle, warm and light with sparks of passion.

As we tucked into bed, I turned to hold her in my arms. She fit in the crook of my body with a precision that was fate in motion. I ran my fingers up and down her arm. Pinpricks of goosebumps followed the pattern of my touch. I loved how her body reacted to me. She nuzzled closer into my arms and sighed, deep and comfortably. I tucked my face into her neck and basked in the scent of her shampoo. My lips took on a mind of their own and left a trail of kisses across her neck and the upper parts of her shoulder. She turned to face me, speaking in a low, quiet tone.

"I don't want to be angry at each other anymore," she whispered.

"Neither do I, Tess. It's all in the past now. This is what matters, right here, right now. I'm sorry I ever lost sight of that," I replied.

She confirmed my sentiments with another kiss. I truly believed every word I said, or at the least I wanted to. Apollo brought an ease back to my life that I thought was gone forever. It brought back my ability to create and to leave my mark on the world. I loved Tess as much as any man had ever loved a woman, but with Apollo I could have it all. I would find a way to keep both. I had to. Holding Tess in my arms, I said a silent vow to protect her from whatever dangers might lurk around the corner for me. I would do everything in my power to shield her from the consequences of my impending path.

For the rest of the night, I put everything else out of my mind: no Apollo, no notes, no drug dealers. I squeezed Tess tightly and placed a gentle kiss on her forehead.

18

Wandering

Lying awake, soaking it all in.
Both happy and sad, where do I begin?
Living a moment you'll never forget.
Living a moment tainted with regret.

"I'm going to find him."

Seth gaped at me in confusion.

"Jamie. I'm going to track him down and get our shipments back on track," I continued.

Not long after the encounter with Pietra Perrault, our last shipment of Apollo hadn't come through. Jamie had been sending over parcels on a regular schedule, always with a high-society guest list attached. Suddenly, there was nothing. Seth and I hadn't thought much of it at first. You don't typically expect drug dealers to be punctual. Jamie had been a welcome surprise in the logistics of our operation, but we knew eventually the wheels would need to be re-greased. We only got suspicious when another week went by with no word. One week late was excusable, but two weeks . . . a mild brew of concern was bubbling up inside me. That's when I had decided to take matters into my own hands.

"Haven't you been looking into this guy for weeks and found next to nothing?" He had gone back to his task, paying little mind to my plan, a clear indication of his perceived success rate.

"I found a name. James Moore."

Seth chuckled innocently, but the insinuation irked me. "Boss, how many James Moores do you think live in New York? Even in Manhattan alone? I don't want to shit all over your grand scheme but, honestly, how the hell are you going to find this guy?"

He was right, of course, but I couldn't let that stop me. We had worked up enough of a roster that we could continue hosting showcase nights for New York's elite, but we only had a small stash of Apollo. I was sure there must be other dealers out there, but in truth, I trusted Jamie. He hadn't led us astray thus far, and that was a hard thing to find. I knew from personal experience that a dependable dealer was one luxury we couldn't afford to take advantage of.

I had to track him down. It was the right thing to do for us and for the studio, at least that was the reason I told myself. I didn't want to admit to myself that I had ulterior motives. Marc's warning of Apollo's consequences haunted my dreams. I was living in constant fear that every blink I took could be my last glimpse of light. I needed to put my mind at ease and Jamie was my best bet at finding the answer.

"I'll find him. You'll see." I was trying to convince myself as much as I was trying to convince Seth, and his soft chuckle in reply proved that he saw through my veiled confidence. Nevertheless, I had to try.

* * *

Washington Square Park is a known hot bed for all the Lower East Side's illicit needs. Some might try to argue that fact, but as someone who should know, this was as good a place to try as any. I sat down on a bench, sipping a water I had bought from a street vendor a few blocks back. I'd been freezing my ass off around most of lower Manhattan for days, hoping that I'd simply happen upon Jamie in a miraculous twist of fate. I should have known better; fate never worked in my favor before.

With my drink nearly finished, I was about to rise from my bench and head home when I saw him from the corner of my eye: James Moore.

He wandered aimlessly through the park, stumbling over branches and stones. I hastily rose from my seat to follow from a safe distance behind. He didn't wander long before trailing off down a dilapidated street that stood out from the rows and rows of brownstone streets, a sad memory of a bygone era.

I ducked behind a nearby stoop and watched Jamie fiddle with a large ring of keys. Every few keys, he paused, a deep gravelly sound erupting from within him. He leaned over with one hand braced against the door of the building. It was the cough of a man who'd spent too many years inhaling everything but oxygen. This dance continued for another few minutes until he finally found the key he sought, shoving it into the lock and disappearing inside.

I scoffed in disbelief, amazed and impressed at my ability to find Jamie in this city of millions. I felt ten feet tall, a man blessed by heaven itself. Maybe fate was on my side after all. My heart was thumping in my chest so loudly I feared Jamie might hear its march from inside his apartment.

I let out a loud, boisterous whoop as soon as I had put enough distance between me and Jamie's apartment. A few passersby glanced at me with confused gazes, but I paid them no mind. I pulled out my cell phone and let the muscle memory in my fingers work their magic as the phone rang.

"Killian? What's up?"

"Tess, you'll never believe—"

I stopped myself before revealing too much. She had always been the one I called when things went right. She was my favorite person to share good news with, but now the words caught in my throat, held back by the blockade of secrets I had created.

"Believe what?" Her voice was earnest and filled with nothing but innocent curiosity.

Guilt flooded my senses and eradicated my pride from seconds ago. "Oh, nothing. I'm just having a good day. The weather is great. Want to join me for a walk?"

"I've got some work to finish up, but how about we take a stroll later? I'll see you around dinner time?"

"Sure thing. See you then."

I shoved the phone back in my pocket, ashamed of my lies, but most of all, ashamed of the path I'd taken to this moment. If tracking down my elusive drug dealer was my biggest thrill in weeks, I feared what future thrills awaited me.

I walked the whole way home that day, my legs sore and my toes frozen by the time I reached our apartment that evening. I had nothing left to give when Tess asked if I still wanted to go for a walk after dinner. All I could say was no.

19

Wrong Answers

Time fades and wounds heal. Eventually she found what was real.
And it led her to ascend with a truer love than any storybook end.

I tracked down Jamie again to a small diner in the heart of Soho. The place was old, having been in business far longer than most of the new residents in this area had been alive. The restaurant was one of the few remnants from the era when lower Manhattan was the grungy part of the city. Trendy coffee shops and shiny luxury brands had paid little mind to this small diner and built around it, slowly closing in on its heritage year over year.

The floors were what I assumed to be a white tile, though their color had been permanently altered by thousands of footsteps. The new color resembled dirty dish water, and I suspected that would be exactly what would come from a thorough scrubbing. The booth cushions, luckily, had not shared the same fate and had been replaced within the last decade. Their glazed navy exterior shimmered in the sunlight, revealing an array of sparkles beneath the surface. They reminded me of something I'd seen in an amusement park, or a themed dining experience, though I couldn't quite place where or when.

I watched the servers bustling around me as I sat in my corner booth, sipping a lukewarm coffee. The taste had a suspicious twinge of dish soap, as if someone hadn't thoroughly washed the pot before refilling. In this moment, however, I was simply thankful to know the pot had been washed at all. A waiter slyly refilled my coffee. In the fraction of time she blocked my eyesight, I lost sight of Jamie. I frantically scanned the room, desperate not to lose him after all the effort I had put into finding him. I turned around in my seat and nearly jumped out of my skin when I came face-to-face with the man I was there to stalk.

"Jamie! I didn't see you there. You practically gave me a heart attack." I tried to laugh away the fact that I had indeed been following him. I hoped my rough acting chops were enough to throw him off my trail.

"Why are you following me?" Jamie asked dryly.

Evidently, my acting needed work.

"I think following is a strong word, but I am happy to see you here—" Jamie slid into the booth with a clamor. His gut bumped into the table, causing the coffee in my mug to slip over the edge with a small, but poignant splash.

"What do you want? Out with it!" I could hear the paranoia in his tone. His head jerked at every minute sound as though the shadows themselves were out to get him. Wide and wild, his eyes flicked back and forth. Finally, he squinted me, but his gaze was distant, as if he was looking through me rather than at me. I realized his eyes were overcast, nearly completed hidden by wispy clouds. He clocked my stare and turned his face away. The questions I had been planning to ask him fell silent.

"It's true then." I lowered my voice to a barely audible whisper. "Apollo users are going blind?"

Jamie scoffed and took the handle of my coffee mug in his grasp. He glanced at me briefly, not even waiting for an approval, before he gulped a large swig. His eyebrows scrunched together, and his nose turned up before skidding the mug back onto the table. It appeared he could taste the soap too.

"I don't know what you think this is, sonny, but we were never dealing with a controlled substance. You and I both knew this had risks. Though a fella must admit, I never anticipated this result. Not even when I was still running with that crowd."

"What do you mean 'when you were running with that crowd'? Are you not dealing anymore?"

He scoffed and reached for the handle of the mug again, stopping himself in better thought before taking another soapy sip. "Has it started yet for you? The blurry vision? The piercing headaches? That's how it went with me. The doctors say my sight won't last through the winter. Even now, I can barely see the hand in front of my face." He gestured innocuously toward his cloudy eyes.

"Still, I'm not blind enough yet that I didn't notice your scrawny ass following me around." He pointed an accusatory finger at me.

When he clocked the terror in my eyes, he softened and laughed dryly to himself. "Sorry, I couldn't help myself."

His chuckle continued for some time before changing into another dry, wheezing cough. He held a napkin over his mouth and tried in vain to keep me from seeing the blood on it. When he abruptly rose from his seat, the table jostled once more, but this time it alluded to something far more sinister than clumsiness.

"Good luck to you, pretty boy. I hope you have a different fate than mine." He turned toward the door, stopping for a moment before reaching into his jacket and pulling out an envelope. My eyes narrowed in on the small white object, taking in its familiar shape and weight. The nearer the envelope came to my hands, the hotter my collar turned. I motioned to grasp it hesitantly between two trembling fingers. Sweat prickled against my hairline. I barely noticed Jamie saunter toward the door, until he walked square into one of the servers on his way, sending dishes and cutlery clattering to the floor. He dashed out onto the street and disappeared into the crowded streets.

My attention returned to the threat in my hands. I gingerly peeled open the flaps of the envelope. As anticipated, its contents were a plain sheet of paper, stiff but even heavier in the words it carried.

Those you love will suffer from your foolishness. Turn back now before it's too late.

20

Partners

I once had a forest. It was wondrous to behold. Then a young man
wandered in, following stories he had been told...

There are some things in life that you know, even as you're experiencing it, that you'll never forget for as long as you live. Tess was the most beautiful bride. At the clinic, Tess wore her hair pinned back and away from her face, but on our wedding day it cascaded around her shoulders. A waterfall on fire, smoldering in the sunlight. I know she had been excited to pick the perfect dress, but I'm embarrassed to admit I couldn't remember a single detail about it. All I remember was staring into her eyes and knowing I would be staring into them for the rest of my life. She was blessed with effortless beauty, the kind that drew envy from all those around her. I saw the other girls stare as she walked down the aisle; Tess simply smiled and waved. As long as I had known her, the beauty of her heart far outshone the beauty of her appearance. She was as perfect as I was flawed.

It rained that day. I suppose rain isn't completely accurate—the heavens erupted on our wedding day. Thunder crackled and boomed through the whole night with lightning following closely behind, ever the accomplice. The entire ceremony had to be moved inside on a dime as the storm cell tore through the venue with little notice. What was once a magical garden party quickly became a cozy night warmed by a fireplace. Tess planned the event for months and was devastated; Not because things hadn't gone how she wanted, but because all the work she put in never came to fruition. I, on the other hand, was grateful for the change of plans. I couldn't have imagined a more perfect day, sitting in a lodge with my gorgeous bride in front of an open fireplace. Being with her was all I had ever wanted. The party never meant much to me.

It was a day of hope, and of everlasting excitement for the future. I wish life had been as easy as we thought it would be on that day. In all our dreaming I never anticipated we would end up here, far removed from the perfect life we envisioned.

I was sure of many things in those early days. Even in my life's most chaotic moments, I always knew where my sail was heading. My art called from distant shores; A siren always beckoning me toward the horizon. It was in the song stuck in my head, forever looping in my brain. When I found Tess, she became the muse I never knew I was lacking. I had never truly painted anything until I found her. Her love showed me the way. She became the song in my head, the one I'd hum aloud without realizing.

Now that everything had gone to shit, she was also the only thing holding me together, which is exactly why I could not lose her. The Fall had already wounded my art, and Apollo was going to hand the final blow. What I thought was once my savior, my way out of this nightmare, had quickly turned into the true nightmare itself. If I lost Tess now too, I'd lose everything. I would lose both my loves, and I knew I couldn't survive that.

I was building up the courage to ask the question I had been dreading ever since Jamie revealed himself in the diner. The minute he had pulled the second envelope from his coat jacket, I knew I had completely misjudged him. The harmless druggie I thought I knew was playing a game in which I was the unwitting pawn. I had been racking my brain trying to figure out what aim he had with the letters. Why had he been trying to scare me off Apollo? I feared I may never know the answer. One thing was certain, this city was no longer safe. I needed an escape; I needed a reprieve from the fear and the unknowns. Even more, I had to keep Tess safe. *Those you love will suffer . . .* The note laid its threat clear, but I would not let it follow through. I was ready to make the right choice, once and for all.

"Tess, honey, do you remember that gallery owner who came to the studio a few weeks ago?"

Tess was unloading groceries in the fridge, her head stuck deep in the back, trying to organize and reorganize the same carton of milk. Persistent as she was, she never had much success in this arena. Usually, some assortment of items from the store simply could not fit inside the fridge no matter how many times she rearranged. She would almost always let out a melodramatic sigh and declare that we would be having the troublesome items for dinner. She let out her trademark huff and emerged from the fridge, placing her hands on her hips and staring at the floor in contemplation. Her foot was tapping out a rhythm of searching as she racked her brain to remember who I was referencing.

"Oh, do you mean the one who wants you to do a special showcase? Wasn't that gallery all the way out in Vegas?"

"Yes, exactly! Yes, that's the one. You know, I've been thinking about it, and I think maybe I should do it . . . " I trailed off, leaving dead air for her to process what I was proposing.

"I thought you weren't interested. You said all those things about it being too far and how New York was the only place you could make it big. What changed?" She momentarily went back to fiddling in the fridge, struck by a moment of organizational inspiration. Her nonchalance surprised me.

"I did say all that. It's true. But I've been thinking that maybe a change of scenery could be good for us. I think it might help me clear out the cobwebs and find some new inspiration."

She had finally given up on the fridge and was watching me explain myself and my sudden change of heart with intent. Her face fell slightly, and she walked over to hold me tightly. Her face nestled into my shoulder, leaving little kisses in its place. She took my face in her hands and stared deeply into my eyes, as if she was wading through the maze of my mind in a single moment.

"Killian, what is really going on here? Is there something you're not telling me?" Her eyes pleaded for the truth, scanning mine for any detection of misdirection.

If there had ever been a moment to come clean, to tell her everything that had happened in the past few months, this was it. There was such earnestness, such purity, in her gaze. I wanted to tell her, to say everything that was pushing up from the back of my throat. Instead, I swallowed the truth, letting it fall to the depths of my empty soul.

Guilt filled my gut as fresh lies fell from my lips. "You can always see right through me," I feigned. "The studio hasn't been doing well since the Fall. We knew business was going to be slow, but I had hoped that after all these special showcases, it would pick up. I think I overestimated the public's ability to move on from everything. I certainly overestimated *my* ability to move on. I haven't been inspired once since the Fall."

Tess grabbed my hand and walked me toward the couch, taking a seat and patting the space beside her. I sat gingerly, avoiding her eyes. I hoped she would take this as a sign of shame, rather than seeing the true betrayal in my words.

"I thought things were getting better. You've done plenty of those shows, and you've been working to the bone to fulfill all the orders. Now there's this showcase offer. It can't be all bad."

"You're right, some good did come from it, but seeing all of my work up on the gallery walls . . . " I trailed off, unable to admit how true these lies were becoming, "It's not the same as before. I'm not proud of anything on those walls, not since the Fall. That's why I didn't want to take the Vegas showcase—I don't deserve it. I didn't want to admit I'm a fraud." Although the words weren't the full truth, they did carry a certain honesty I hadn't allowed myself to reveal for a long while now. I had been uninspired, but my solution wasn't a spontaneous trip to Las Vegas. I wish it had been.

She pondered me for a moment before dropping her head in consideration. Chewing her bottom lip as the wheels in her head churned. I could never read her 'pondering face.' She was perfect as a clinic aide because she never revealed her true emotions. She could listen to tales of heartbreak or incredible adventure without ever showing a sign of emotion. It was always curious to me that a woman with such a fiery temper could be stoic and reserved in her place of work. I always wondered how she was able to turn off the faucet of emotion I knew hid behind her stoic expression.

Seeing her in this ambiguous state of contemplation reminded me of when we had first met. She held her cards close to her chest even then, never revealing that she was interested in me too until I was finally a free man.

"Let's do it," she said after her long deliberation, a smile lighting up her whole face as she leaned in for a quick kiss.

To say I was surprised was a gross understatement. Tess had an incredible career here in New York. She went to work at her dream job every day. Asking her to leave it all behind would have been painfully selfish of me, if it wasn't for her that I was asking. I couldn't imagine why she agreed to go.

"Honey, are you sure? You'd have to leave the clinic. I know how much you adore your job."

"The clinic is a dream for me, but you're the love of my life. You're my partner and I would do anything for you. If you need to go, then my only choice is to go with you." She said those words with such certainty. I envied her confidence. She was always sure of herself and her choices.

Her selfless confidence gave me the courage to follow through on what I knew was the right choice. Ever since Apollo had fallen into my lap, I had been a slave to its whims. I was walking a path backward toward my darkest days. I knew this and yet I was terrified to let it go. After my encounter with Jamie, the road before me was illuminated in lurid light. If I didn't stop, if I didn't leave this all behind, I wasn't just giving up my sobriety, I was giving up my future.

I already lost the privilege of seeing her stunning beauty in full luminescence. I couldn't give up the chance to ever see her again. It was my turn to protect her from the dangers of the world, though she didn't know it. This was the only road forward now. I would keep her safe, no matter the cost.

* * *

I've never been one for goodbyes. There was too much pressure in a goodbye, far more than the dreaded first impression. First impressions can be wrong, can be rectified, but a goodbye lasts forever. It is the moment you will remember after everything else fades away. My parents' funeral was my first real experience with the finality of a goodbye. A eulogy is a cruel task for a nine-year-old boy. I hadn't even hit puberty but was charged with sharing aloud the complexities of my relationship with the people who gave me life but never let me live it. Even after all these years, I still couldn't properly describe the difficult emotions that accompany memories of my parents.

That day was one of the worst of my life and it wasn't because of the loss I should have been consumed by. I was all too aware it was obvious that I didn't miss them in the least. Since that day, I'd worked to bury my emotions deep down and never let anyone see what I didn't want them to. I became one of the perfectly curated paintings I'd spent my life creating.

Sometimes I envied those who had a so-called 'happy childhood,' but I think that past trauma only led me closer to finding my real family. I had built a life I was proud of, and even more, a home that truly satisfied me. Yet, there I was, about to tear it all down.

I stood still in a sea of city activity. People swam around me impatiently, eager to get wherever they were going. They shouted for me to move, to get out of their way, but as I stared at the office I had shaped into a home, my world fell silent. Inside lay my studio, my single greatest achievement since moving to the city. It wasn't a small feat for an independent artist to hold a lease on their own gallery in the city. This was a tough business, but I had survived all the hurdles it had ever thrown at me. All but one.

* * *

"I hope now you understand why I have to go." I avoided Seth's eyes, absentmindedly shuffling paintbrushes and sketchbooks from my desk. I had laid bare everything I learned from

Jamie, the notes, the blindness, everything. It broke my heart watching Seth's face drop as he put together the hidden meaning in my words.

"I guess this means I have to find a new job." Seth shuffled around the studio; his head bent. He languished in his pity for only a few moments before dawning a newfound confidence, putting on a brave face as he strode over, hand extended. He may have worked up the courage to face me, but his trembling lip gave him away. "It's been an honor working for you, boss-," he stopped and chuckled unconvincingly, "guess this is the last time I get to call you that."

Thankfully, I knew something he didn't.

"You're right, Seth, I think it is time you find a new job. Luckily, I'm in need of a studio manager to keep an eye on things while I'm away and you come highly recommended."

Confusion cast a shadow over his eyes until realization shone a new light on them. His hand, still extended, wavered and dropped before he launched into a full-blown hug. "I won't let you down, sir. Business will be better than ever before! I guarantee it."

His smile was infectious. It filled my heart with joy, a welcome surprise to my dread before coming here today. This may have been a goodbye, but at least it was the happy kind. "I know you're the right man for the job, Seth. You're going to do great."

I left him with a brief pat on the shoulder before grabbing a handful of items from my desk and turning to leave. The boy practically jumped for joy behind me as I reached the door. It was bittersweet leaving the studio, but I meant what I said to Seth. This place was in good hands.

I left him with a few departing words before closing the door on that chapter of my life. "One last thing, Seth. I think it's about time you drop the 'Boss' and call me Killian. We are partners now, after all."

21

Ripples

You hide behind your eyes. They're a symbol of your lies.
You should never have to be alone, but it's all you've ever known.
You hide behind your eyes. Their secrets will be your demise.

It was morning. Our last morning in New York.

The air was heavy with anticipation of events yet to happen. We had a fresh start ahead, and I was eager not to squander the opportunity.

I lay there next to Tess, basking in her intoxicating light. Her hair was spread across her face in a beautiful tableau. She was gorgeous. Her cheekbones were high, her hips were slender, and her soul was unnaturally pure. A stray lock of hair fell carelessly across her eyelids, peeking through her lashes as they gently fluttered. I wondered what an angel dreamed of. Seeing her in the early sunlight—I couldn't imagine a more perfect sight on earth. I brushed the stray hair from her face, trailing my thumb along her skin. I drank in the moment. I made a new pact with myself. I would no longer try to impress a world that was not listening. All that truly matters in this life is making sure you matter to at least one person. She was my person.

Even before the Fall I feared I had taken too much of our time together for granted. There was always something more important than her. I'd been a fool. Leaving New York had reminded me of a lesson I'd learned many times before: our time on this earth is finite. My father taught me that. He taught me many things, of course, chief among them to hide my emotions. I always thought that was my strength, but life's recent events made me wonder if I was doomed to repeat the mistakes of my father. I made a habit of not thinking too hard about how my life might have turned out had my parent's car reached its destination that night.

"Killian," Tess whispered.

Her voice brought me back from my memories. She was awake now, peering up at me through squinting eyes. She stretched out her arms, wrapping them around me.

"Where were you?" she asked. Her thumb caressed the nape of my neck. I closed my eyes and leaned into her touch.

"I was thinking about my grandfather. I wish you could have met him."

"Me too." She smiled, dusting the sleep from her eyes. "Will you tell me about him?"

"What do you want to know?" I brushed the mischievous hair from her face as she yawned, stretching her arms wide toward the sky.

"Everything," she said. "Start at the beginning."

My grandfather was a fisherman off the Gulf Coast of Louisiana. He made his living dredging up oysters, shrimp and crayfish that his wealthy neighbors would gorge themselves sick on in their southern mansions. He woke each morning at 3 a.m. to take the boat out and bring in a catch for the morning markets. He worked long, grueling hours, but it was simple work, and he enjoyed the solitude. When he was on the boat, it was just him, the marsh and the sunrise.

The day my father was born, he was slated to join the family business. From the time he was old enough to see over the steering wheel, he'd accompany my grandfather on the boat each morning before school. He learned how to cast the nets, where to fish for a good catch, and how to haggle for a fair price. To my grandfather, there was never any possibility for a different path.

My father, on the other hand, never wanted to be a part of the fisherman's life. He loathed the quiet and the damp that followed them around like a stray dog. Early mornings brought him no peace and the cranky port men only added to his misery. Above all else, he hated my grandfather for deciding his fate. The day my father graduated from high school he vowed to never so much as look at a boat again. He believed that if he even stepped one foot on that fishing rig, he'd be condemned to living his whole life on it. He was probably right.

So, he ran away the summer after graduation. He packed up his things early in the morning and left before the sun came up, it was the only early morning he'd enjoyed in his whole life. On his way out the door he passed my grandfather, sitting on the front porch in a rocking chair. The way Granddad tells the story, they didn't exchange a single word before my father walked off into the sunrise. Even as a boy, I believed there was more to that story, but I never got up the courage to ask him about it.

"What happened then?" she asked.

"I don't know much about my father's early days in the city, he never dared speak about a time when he wasn't already successful. As a kid he made it out as if he simply knocked on the door of the first investment banker he found and got himself an internship. Neither would have admitted it, but dad and Granddad had a similar habit of leaving out certain, unfavorable, details in their stories."

"Do you think it could have been that easy for him?"

I considered for a moment, truly wondering if my father had stumbled upon the best luck in New York City. "Dad always did have a way with numbers. He also had a keen sense for bullshit and a low tolerance for stupidity. In the handful of years since he had left home, my father became one of the rich assholes slurping oysters he'd been raised to hate. It was clear to me even as a child that everything my father did was to spite his own father. He had no passion for banking, nor did he enjoy the company of the legacy stockbrokers he spent every day with. He grew to love it for no other reason than vengeance. Knowing his own father would hate the man he had become was all the motivation he needed.

"I've spent many nights imagining the two of them sitting down together, finding common ground and setting aside their childish stubbornness. I pictured a perfect scene in which they'd discover they had more in common than they realized and found a way to coexist. I imagine the two worlds I was raised in becoming one."

"When did you go to live with your grandparents?"

"I was nine when the accident happened."

She shifted, sitting up straighter. "You've never told me what happened that night."

I sighed, rubbing my fingers against my temples, trying to remember the event I'd spent years trying to forget.

"You don't have to tell me if you don't want to. I want you to know that." Her eyes pierced into my soul, begging to be let inside.

"It's okay. I want to, but it's difficult to talk about," I said in honesty.

After a few minutes of collecting myself, I continued. "My father got a late-night phone call at our Hampton home. He never said who it was or what he talked about and to this day I still don't know. I remember my mother coming into my room, saying that we had to go back to the city. It was still dark out and I was barely awake as she gathered my things and strapped me into the backseat of our car. We weren't driving for more than a few minutes before I fell asleep again. Maybe it was the dark, maybe the roads were wet, maybe he was distracted from that mysterious phone call, but whatever the reason my father lost control of the car. I was woken up by this beastly howl. It was such a strange noise. I'll never forget it. It was a symphony of the worst sounds imaginable: glass bursting into a million pieces, tires squealing on the road, and metal contorting as we pierced the guardrails. Then it all went silent as we plunged into the water. As we fell deeper, the silence only grew until it washed us all away. I was the only one who resurfaced."

I chuckled at the irony of the situation. "The water is what had driven two generations of my family's men apart and it is what would keep them apart for eternity."

Tess reached over, clasping her hand in mine. She squeezed tightly, urging me to continue. I appreciated her urging, but I was surprised that I didn't need it. The story I hadn't ever told was now flooding from my mouth.

"After the accident, I went to live with the grandparents I had never met. I spent most of those first few weeks hiding in the room my father had grown up in. I was terrified of the water that taunted me all around the house. I filled my days searching through closets and discovering the secrets my father had stashed under that same bed many years ago. I learned more about him in those few weeks than I did the whole time he was alive. He never spoke of growing up in Louisiana, but suddenly I had a window into his childhood.

"I awoke one morning before dawn. My grandfather was standing above me wearing a bright yellow rain jacket and large, bulking galoshes. In his hands he held a matching set to his own, only much smaller. From that morning on he took me out on the rig and taught me how to fish. He helped me through my fear of the water, offering me safety I had never felt with my own father. We would talk about everything from cracker jack toys to Greek philosophy. Granddad was surprisingly well read on the works of Plato. He was a good man, but stern. He didn't have time for bullshit and always made time for family. I learned a lot about life from him. Both my father and him shared the same core sentiment which they instilled in me: nothing in life is ever given, it must be taken. As hard as we try to point our sails toward our heading, we will always be subject to the fates of the tide and the wind.

"When my own graduation came and went, I chose to leave as my father had, but this time I had Granddad's blessing."

"When did he pass?"

"Not long after I got to New York. I miss him every day, but I am glad he never had to see my darker years."

She pressed her forehead against mine. "He would be proud of you, Killian. I know I am."

I hoped that was true.

22

Welcome Home

She ran from the place she had always called home to meet a person she had never really known. She figured out the answer, but the question stilled loomed: What if this person is not yet in bloom?

Las Vegas isn't all that different from New York, I'd come to discover. It's loud and messy and chaotic, filled with crowds of people, all wanting something different from you. One of the comforting things about New York was that there was always someone crazier than you on the street. Vegas was no different. Even in the boisterousness, it was easy to fade into the shadows and become a faceless spectator. I'd traveled across the country and yet the game was the same. The players had changed, but the rules remained. The only true difference was the heat.

New York had many flaws. It was a city that was self-obsessed and selfish. It found new ways to break you down, eating away at you bit by bit, slow enough you don't even realize how you'd changed. And yet, it was home. It was the place Tess and I built a life together. It was where I first found my voice and learned to use it. The city was a comfort, despite all its discomfort. I took solace in the fact that Las Vegas is just a warmer, sunnier reflection of the city that raised me. In the dark of the night, when the lights shined brightest and the heat hid, I'd close my eyes, imagining I was back in New York. The veil thinned and I was transported back home. Despite the aching for the familiarity of our old lives, it didn't take long for us to settle into our new routine.

For the first time in our marriage, Tess and I were living in a floor plan larger than 600 sq. ft. The rental home we secured was a staggering, three-level bungalow, complete with a garage and a patio. The extra space was closing the distance between us. The change in scenery reflected an immediate shift in the both of us. We were reverting to happier versions of ourselves, finding bits and pieces of each other that had been lost along the way. I felt different here. I rose early in the mornings with anticipation and hope for a new day. Tess was changing too; she laughed more, finding levity and joy in life's smaller moments once more. I hoped this move would be the final piece in bringing us back together, but I knew deep down that a house could only do so much.

The back patio brought cool sun in the mornings, and was covered by shade after lunch, keeping it at a pleasant, mild temperature and the perfect spot for quiet contemplation. I sat facing a blank canvas propped on an easel. I watched it from my seat, focusing on its details. My eyes walked over every crease and bump, trying to find some tangible reasoning for why I could not bring myself to paint it. The glass of iced tea I'd poured hours ago had developed a ring of condensation, leaving a sizable puddle in its wake when I finally took my first sip. The heat was unyielding in every aspect, from the simplest act of melting ice to the more complex of changing my mind. There was nowhere to hide in the desert and as I stared at the empty canvas, I became less certain of the choices I had made in New York.

When we left the city, I promised myself I would be done with Apollo, but the desert's heat was a pressure cooker. The fear crept back in, knotting my stomach and giving voice to the devil residing in my mind, 'What if you're not good enough without it?'

Tess walked toward me with a fresh drink in her hand. Her eyes were covered by a large, floppy sun hat, a new style she had become quite fond of in our short desert respite. Shadows hid most of her face, but her wide smile gave her away. She walked closer to me, a smirk taking the place of her smile, "Mind if I join you?"

I motioned to the empty chair to my left, eager for her to join me and even more eager to be free of my thoughts. She walked past the open chair and nestled onto my lap, wrapping her arms around my neck. I shivered as a bead of condensation from her glass slid down the back of my neck. She chuckled at my reaction and kissed me on the cheek before resting her head on my shoulder.

"I think this is some of your best work Mr. St. James."

"If you must know, *Mrs. St. James,* it's still a work in progress."

"Doesn't look very in progress to me," she mumbled, not trying to hide her sarcasm.

I narrowed my eyes at her, inciting a round of boisterous laughter in us both. When she finally regained her composure her voice softened, "What's going on in that beautiful brain of yours?"

Her eyes were warm with genuine interest. This was the moment. If I was going to come clean, there would be no better time than now. My heart rate quickened in anticipation. I toyed with the words in my mouth, imagining how they would spill out and finally be free in the world.

The silence beckoned me to speak, but nothing came out.

My heart steadied, knowing before my mind did that I'd lost the courage.

"I want to be better here. I *need* to be better, for you." It was the truth but only a shard of it.

"My love," Tess tilted my chin to meet her eyes, peering into the deepest parts of my soul, "You need to let go of this pressure you put on yourself. Your drive is one of the many things I admire about you, but this is a chance for us to leave the past behind. I want to take that chance, don't you?"

"Yes, of course I do."

"Good, then it's settled. Yesterday is gone, it can't hurt us anymore. Today is all that matters, and I want to spend it with you."

She kissed me then, and with her kiss she said everything else that I needed to know.

* * *

The empty canvas still sat atop the easel on the patio though it was now close to midnight. I stood at the bedroom window, watching it in aimless thought as I had that afternoon. I had woken from my dreamless sleep, still tormented by the devil's words playing in my head and fighting for dominance within my heart. I wanted to give in to Tess's pleas, to start fresh and leave Apollo behind me, but fear is a fierce, unrelenting adversary, even for love.

I dug for the small piece of paper that I knew was stored somewhere in my wallet. I'd forgotten about it in the months since it first found its home there, but now my fingers absentmindedly dialed the numbers in fine print. The dial tone rang.

"Hello?"

"Edgar—It's Killian."

"Oh, Killian! I'm glad to hear from you, even at this hour." He let out a chuckle that evolved into a cough. "What's on your mind?"

He didn't miss a beat. His lack of questioning was an immense relief. My mind eased, knowing it had made the right decision to call him. "I have a choice to make, and I don't know what to do. I'm worried I'm going to mess everything up."

He waited, letting the silence do most of the talking for him. "Killian, if you're hoping I'm going to make this choice for you, you've got another thing coming. The only person who can make your choices is you."

"But how will I know it's the right path?"

"You can't, not for sure, but I have a suspicion you know what's right. You wouldn't be so worried if you didn't."

His words brought tears to my eyes, which now streamed down my face, one burning drop after the other. I wiped them away with the back of my hand, sniffling to regain my composure, "You hardly know me. Do you have that much faith in me?" I asked.

"I do. It's true that you and I don't know each other well, but I can tell when a person has their internal compass pointed in the right direction. You'll know what's right. You only need to find the courage to make the choice."

He didn't linger long after that. He didn't need to. After we hung up the phone, I loitered by the windowsill. I replayed his words, trying to hold back the violent whispers that ran wild in the back of my mind.

I was finally ready to uphold what I had vowed on the other side of the country. Effectuation stepped into the moonlight light, greeting me like an old friend. I was not anxious from its arrival, but ready to listen. It was time to let go.

Apollo was a reminder of the past, of all that I had lost and all I would never achieve. It was a barrier to the future, holding me back from embracing this new world. I couldn't say exactly how, but I knew I would find new beauty in a gray world, Tess was living proof of that. Her beauty was iridescent even without its hue. I would find new springs of inspiration, I was sure, but until that day she would be my bedrock, the support I needed until I could stand on my own. She had been all along; I'd been too blind to see it.

I thought toward the approaching dawn, hoping Pietra would understand my new path. Apollo would only bring more heartache to already suffering people. I could see that clearly now and I couldn't be a part of it anymore. It broke my heart to know that my art, the works I had only ever intended to bring others joy, could perpetrate such despair. Apollo had twisted what was once pure into a vessel for destruction, but in its own way it guided me to the answer I'd forgotten I already knew.

My wife was the only crutch I ever needed to get through the Fall, to get through anything. Not Apollo, not Jamie, not Pietra, not even my art. Tomorrow I was going to make the right choices, the choices I should have made all those months ago, choices I could be proud to make. Tomorrow everything was going to change.

23

Revelations

Terrified of holding on too tight.
Terrified because the end is in sight.
Both happy and sad as the lights dim low.
Lying awake, where did it all go?

The beautiful thing about good lighting is that it can completely change your point of view. It's a common misconception that color is the most defining part of an image, but I learned early on that was a myth. Without proper lighting, nothing could truly come to life. This was all the more evident under the Nevada sun. I was back to living a kosher life of black and white, but the constant sunshine helped to lighten the loss of color. The bright gleams of the light brought new life and texture to every sight, something New York was never able to provide. The glow against my skin was good for me. I was inspired, truly inspired for the first time since the Fall.

I woke up early, not a difficult feat with the desert light filtering in through our curtain-less windows, and came to Pietra's studio in a fit of creativity. As the creation on canvas took shape before me, my emotions chased each other in a vicious battle for victory. Nerves, excitement, dread, and hope all battled for first place. I was back at the precipice of my journey as an artist, not quite knowing what would come from my brush on paper. Part of me still believed the best of my works were behind me. I feared I would never create anything truly great again. But for this one morning, the fears ebbed back, and passion won out.

"You're here early."

I hadn't noticed Pietra walk into the studio. I assumed she had been there for a while, judging by her mostly empty mug of coffee. It was polite of her to avoid interrupting me, but it was unsettling to know she had been watching me. Anticipation quickly took over as she approached the easel. I wanted her to approve of this latest work, more than as the person funding my paycheck. I respected Pietra and what she had built in Vegas. She had a keen eye for talent, and I was humbled by her offer to show my paintings in her gallery. I wanted my career to reach its peak again, but more than that I wanted to be worthy of my success. I wanted someone to gaze upon my work in awe. I wanted to prove to myself that I still had it, even after the Fall, even without Apollo, I was enough.

"Huh." Pietra stared deeply into the canvas.

She wore glasses today. The thin gold frames circled her eyes and matched her complexion. Paired with her loose, satin shirt and flowing trousers, she yet again toed the line between high fashion and executive prowess. No matter the setting there was no mistaking the woman had excellent taste and enough money to prove it. She sipped her nearly empty coffee mug, her face perfectly poised with not a muscle out of place, but her white knuckled grip told a different story from her effortless exterior.

"Killian, can I be honest with you?" She turned and gracefully lowered herself into a nearby armchair, bringing her other hand to cradle the mug, intensifying her hold. "This isn't your best work. It's good, don't get me wrong, but it's not what I was hoping for."

My heart sank.

"Do you know why I offered you this residency?" She leaned forward, her elbows resting on her knees. Her blouse puckered, giving a glimpse of the crystal skin that lay beneath. The way she moved was practiced and poised, a calculated pose that, I assumed, made it easier for her to take dominance in any conversation. I pulled my eyes away from her ploy and met the smirk spreading across her lips.

"Let me answer that for you. You're a talented painter, there's no denying, but what I saw in New York . . ." She trailed off. "Why do you think I was so taken with your work?" She gave me a pointed stare.

"I know what you're going to say, Pietra. You brought me out here for more exclusive showcases, but can't you see what Apollo is doing to people? It isn't right."

Her polished exterior cracked in an instant. "You don't think I know what it does?"

She slammed the coffee mug onto a side table. "Do you think these glasses are for show, St. James?" She whipped off the lenses and held them tightly between her fingertips. "I know damn well what the cost is."

She calmed slightly at this confession, panting out her anger, but her steely gaze returned to meet mine once more as she spoke her final threat. "Now, here's what is going to happen next. You're going to toss out that garbage." She gestured to the canvas then tossed a bag of Apollo in my lap. "Then you're going to take a great big hit of *that* and paint me something I can actually fucking sell."

Her voice was venomously stoic as she delivered the final blow. Despite the involuntary chills that ran down my spine, her controlled demands only stoked the defiant fire inside me. I've never been good at taking orders.

I folded the bag into my palm met Pietra's gaze dead in the eyes. "I've given this up and you should too. We can move on from Apollo, together. I'll paint you a few more pieces to fill the gallery. You'll see, it doesn't have to be this way."

I stood and moved toward the door. A hand grabbed my shoulder. I turned, expecting an apology, or at the least understanding resignation. Instead, I was taken aback by a searing pain radiating across my right cheek. It rippled through my face sending tendrils behind my eyes and through my nose. The air in my lungs escaped rapidly in a ragged cough as my eyes watered.

"Do you truly have the gall to believe that you're special? What did you think was going to happen here? You'd give your self-righteous speech, and I would blindly accept that you simply don't 'feel like it' anymore?

"You are right in one aspect, Killian. You are special, but not because of your talent. I needed a way to keep my gallery alive and by heavens I found one. It wasn't a coincidence that brute of a beast Jamie dropped his stash in your studio. I did my research on you. I never make an investment I can't back up with stone cold facts. A tortured artist with a murky past, a shadowy drug problem and *painfully* obvious daddy issues? I mean come on; it was too easy!" She was shouting now, pacing dangerously around the room.

It wasn't until that moment, watching her stalking me from the corners of the studio, that I realized I had misjudged Pietra completely. For the first time in my life, fear consumed me. I was not the one in control. All this time I thought Jamie was the mastermind, but as I stared at Pietra's bulging eyes, I saw the truth: This was her game, and I was only a pawn. Raw power glared back at me, blood on her mind.

I straightened myself out from her blow, shielding my face from her hands but not daring to lose her from my sight. I mustered as much strength as I had to steadily deliver, "We're done here."

"Fine!" She hissed back at me, "You've made your choice. But I know you and I know how this ends. You won't be able to resist this life for long. That adorable little wife of yours might have been able to sway you for now, but you and I both know you need more. You need more than she can ever give you. You need Apollo and you need me!"

I scurried through the door, darting into the blinding light of the desert. I stumbled through the crowd that passed in front of Pietra's studio, fear threatened to cripple me with each backward glance. I wanted to believe I was stronger than she claimed, but that bag of Apollo in my pocket beckoned me. For all her sins, she hadn't been wrong yet.

24

Choices

The storms stops. They always do. And again she sees that stream of sunlight. But this time, she hesitates. The storm will come. Should she even dare to touch the sun?

This had gone on long enough. It was time to tell Tess everything. I should have told her the second I discovered Apollo. She deserved to know the truth about my showcases. I hadn't even been honest about why we moved here and now she was in danger from a force she didn't know existed. Pietra proved today that she was many things, unpredictable and manipulative, but chief among them was dangerous. She had orchestrated this whole ordeal to suit her own selfish desires. I didn't want to know what she was willing to do to someone who had wronged her. I'd stepped out of the ring mid-fight, but I wasn't naive enough to believe there wouldn't be consequences. The time of reckoning was upon us, and I needed to come clean—about everything—before it was too late.

I was greeted by the brisk coolness of the kitchen. Its shimmering stainless steel glared back at me, stopping me mid-step.

My eyes wandered their surroundings with a perilous caution. The air was heavy with anticipation and heartache. I couldn't discern why, but I was compelled to take stock of every sight before me. I worried it would crumble before my eyes. As they scanned their horizons, my eyes picked up on what my mind had confused—the room provoked me with such an earnest angst. Its spotless white tiles littered the floors. Faceless panels reflected shining gray metal lining every appliance, drawer and cabinet.

A sudden thought interrupted this one-man showdown with my soulless opponent. The thought was bright and colorful. It radiated warmth and love. The thought was filled with deep reds, powerful oranges, and vibrant, but not lurid, yellows. The thought was everything this home was not. The thought interrupted my silent feud with the kitchen and sent me wandering through the empty hallways of fine furniture.

"Tess?" I called into the emptiness. I stared apprehensively at our bedroom, tentative for reasons I couldn't place. My body moved with a slow caution that only it could perceive, my mind stayed alert with arrogant ignorance. The vast room loomed ahead, calling out in shrieks of pain. The paint-less walls sent out blood-curdling screams of fear, but the true horror was the faint whisper of a whimper wafting from the washroom up the stairs. I trod the steps, repeating my call into the emptiness. "Tess?"

I opened the door with a meager push, terrified of what I might find. The washroom itself was undisturbed, a mirror to the rest of the colorless house. Except in the corner of this room, a huddled figure greeted me. She cried fiercely into herself, face hidden behind a waterfall.

"Tess?" I cooed as calmly as I could muster, my voice a humble hand reaching toward the shuddering girl. She shuddered. Her hopeful eyes met my own perplexed ones and I realized her cries were not ones of angst or hurt, but of joy.

She spoke swiftly, "Killian, I'm pregnant."

It was barely more than a whisper, but with those three words, my soul collapses and unites at once. A symphony roared through me as I came to join her on the floor in a huddle. Everything else fell away as I brought her into my arms and joined in her song. My skin burned and my eyes filled with tears. Before those simple but monumental words, I truly believed I would never be a father. I had never wanted to be a father, to follow that path, and yet—in this soulless house—we created life.

Flashes of a future I never thought I wanted filled my mind. Scratches and dents embellish dark wood cabinets. The floors are worn with years of small feet running through life. Sunlight shines through open windows as memories are served from the table engraved with family stories. The realization is jolting and traumatic.

It became overwhelmingly clear. This child would be my crowning achievement—that is what my legacy would be. I had been chasing the wrong thing all along. I had lost my art, but this child could be everything I would never become. It would be my prize, my—

"Killian, are you happy?" Her eyes saw through me, reflection pools of my own worst fears. Still, she clung to me with a hopeful smile. She couldn't have known that this news came at the exact moment I put us all in danger. Those words changed everything.

"Tess, of course, I—" The words caught in my throat, blocked by an intruder I'd come to know far too well. I stumbled, trying to somersault those words out of my mouth, to give her the reassurance that I was happy. I was more than happy. I was . . . no. I was afraid.

Everything stopped at that moment. Fear had climbed inside my body and pushed me out of control. I saw myself, still holding the woman I love as she silently pleaded for my answer. I stared down at her, dumbfounded and shaken. My eyes grew wide, and my head shook rapidly until my whole body was quivering. Tess shuffled away from me, frightened at the sudden shift in reaction. It was as if I was a bystander in my own body and fear was holding the reins. I stumbled upright and turned to run. Tess called out, desperately trying to bait my body back, but I was unresponsive. I peddled down the staircase, falling over each step as if I had at that very moment, learned to walk. I supposed in some ways I had; fear had never driven this vehicle before.

I followed my body, tripping and toppling its way into the car it had come from mere minutes ago. How had everything gone to shit in that short time? My world had been both enlightened and thrust into darkness, and yet the engine was still warm. My fingers absentmindedly found their way to the glove compartment and blindly thrashed about, scattering its contents across the interior, searching for their familiar friend.

They came up empty. I had forgotten that I'd cleared out my stash when we moved. I gripped the steering wheel until my knuckles turned white and screamed. I let out the sound I wanted to release for far too long. It was a sound of agony and of sorrow. It took everything else from my body leaving me numb in the silence.

I thrust my head forward, bringing forth a small chirp from the horn as it hit the wheel. I heaved a sob from my chest. Hot tears welled and blurred my eyes. That's when I heard it. The tiniest noise. The faintest sound of plastic wrinkling. I still had the bag Pietra threw at me.

I snatched the small, clear parcel with such force, my fingernails dug back into my own hand, leaving small indents behind as a reminder. I was alarmed to find the sensation was comforting. It distracted me from the pain in my heart. I pressed my fingers to my palms once more, relishing the brief distraction. My body convulsed from the power of it. My eyes filled with yet more tears, now brought on by shame, as I filled and rolled the familiar drug that doomed me from the start.

I took hit after hit, desperate for the effects to take over. Pietra had won. I would play her game. I had to. Tess's words had both opened a door to a new life and simultaneously locked me into my darkest fears. I would not—I *could* not endanger this child with my righteous indignation. There was no allowance for piety when legacy was on the line.

I brushed away the ash from the spent half roll as my foot landed on the gas with a heavy impact. I swerved through the streets, chasing the colors flying through my mind. The blazing lights served as my guide. They were leading me back to the scene of my crimes. It was time to hang my head in defeat and give in to the ulterior motives of my oppressor.

I rocketed around corners, swerving in and out of lanes. I held down the horn as unsuspecting drivers fell quickly behind me. The effects of Apollo grew more intense by the second, the colors of the Las Vegas strip blurring all around me. I was pulled into their trance, entering a state of ecstasy I hadn't yet achieved.

I watched them swirl through each other as I registered a silent weightlessness.

Everything went still for a single second. Barely long enough for a thought to register. *I might have taken too much.*

I had taken in too much of everything, the fear, the guilt, the color, the sound. It all fell together as gravity took back control.

The sound was blinding.

* * *

He had been here before. Once upon a time, a small boy sat where the man sat now. Glass fell in peaceful shards of crystal all around him. The lights of the city illuminated his spiral, allowing him to watch it all play out in front of him.

He's older now but finds himself crawling from a familiar wreckage, however this is one of his own design. He emerges at the edge of the Nevada Desert. Its barren landscape was an ironic welcome to the turmoil inside his head.

The steaming air squeezes his throat as he sheds his suit coat. His shoes are scuffed in seconds of his mindless blundering through the burning sand.

His hands stand quivering as he continues his pilgrimage onto the horizon. He locks his eyes to the setting sun, fearing if he doesn't, he won't see it again. He was going to come clean. He was going to tell her everything; that was his intention, at least. He fell apart the moment he saw her face.

The worthless coward ran from the woman he loves in her time of need. He ran back to the drug he swore he would never return to. Apollo: it had infused itself into his life, giving him back his sight. But the devil never makes deals without a price. He had been on a precipice and now he was ready to step off the ledge. He would give up everything for Tess, even his soul. It was only his faith in her love for him that eased his fears. Yes, he would submit to Pietra to save his family.

Family. The word struck him in the chaos of the moment. His brainless stumble halted for a moment as he processed this new word. Up until now, it was only the two of them. A unit, yes, but not quite a family, not until now. He had finally achieved the life he never knew he wanted but he would never have the chance to see it.

It has always been said that the love between a child and parent is unconditional. The prevailing theory is that children will love their parents even when they hate them. But Killian lived through proof that this was unequivocally false. Love was a choice, and no child could ever love a man who only wanted for himself. He was selfish. He was cowardly. He fell to temptation to feed his own ego. He thought of no one when he took that first hit.

That was the tipping point. That was the moment that changed his life forever and he had taken that step out of spite. What a terrible reason for ruining a life. That one choice thrust him into this current moment. That one choice had destroyed everything.

Who was he now? A failed artist, only worth what Apollo was able to provide. An ignorant man, too blinded by his own ego to see the danger that lured him here in the first place. A coward who would submit to a tyrant at the first sign of struggle. That was a man who didn't deserve unconditional love.

So, he retreated into the darkness, to the drug that brought him light. The small plastic bag containing the Apollo leaves, shielded from him by the fabric of his jeans, crinkles and curls with every step. These simple leaves and paper weigh on him as gravity weighs on the earth; they constantly remind him of the burden he carries.

His hands found their way to his midnight hair as they tear through the gelled strands with a ferocious zest, determined to find some source of satisfaction. His fingers gouged into his crown, desperately imploring relief from the crushing pain. He pulled and scratched, determined to rip away an invisible itch. His fingers paled in comparison to the nails he yearned to pound into his head.

Why was it that physical pain could never encapsulate emotional sorrow? No matter how much the body stung, it could never hurt as much as *feeling* could. As much as he wished he could claw away the anguish, the shame, he knew it would never be enough.

He stopped, suddenly sated with his separation from the city of stolen dreams. It was as if he was living life on fast forward. Before he even blinked, his fingers slipped into the familiar movements.

Another blink. His lips clenched the cylinder as his fingers flipped open the lighter he'd kept near his heart for years. He gazed down at the familiar inscription with a fond memory. Though his eyes were no longer strong enough to read it, his thumb ran over the embossed words he wished were still true.

To Killian, with love forever–Tess

The sentimental flame ignited his only chance at a conventional existence. He knew this was the only relief he would find. Tess used to be his source of light, of clarity and ease, but he'd ruined that now. Apollo was all he had left.

His vision brightened, as it did with every puff that came be-fore. The foggy dullness of the setting sun became crisp once more. He could see every wisp of a cloud and every grain of sand beneath his feet. Then the shades of gray encroaching on his vision, one by one, became vibrant colors.

Arriving in a slow steady marching line, red was the first to come out of hiding, the color of his beloved Tess's hair. The color he once equated with love took its rightful place on the throne of anger. It reminded him of everything he failed to be for her. He turned away from red, eager to find another color to qualm his memories.

Orange followed, then yellow. More marched along in line until Killian's sight reached full iridescence. He inhaled more of the miracle madness and exhaled a pant of disgrace. If he were a stronger man, he would have been able to resist this.

His screams echoed back to him through the barren desert. "You're a fool, Killian, a damned fool. Whoever said you deserved to see your child's first steps? Who said you had a right to keep this wretched secret? She will never forgive you for this." His one-man war ended in a racking sob that could only be described as true pain. His body emoted pure and profound passion until, violently, it stopped.

Something was wrong.

His vision blurred. The colors faded, all of them gone too quickly. He was left in darkness, screaming. This was not supposed to happen, not yet.

The thoughts in his mind charged toward each other in an endless battlefield as Killian was compelled to the ground by his weakened knees. Shuddering and moaning, his lanky legs folded beneath him haphazardly. His arms curled around his head, attempting to protect any sliver of unadulterated dignity.

He dangled off the ledge, held in place by only his smooth fingers, never roughed by nature's cruel will, but it was not enough. The last thing he heard before the abyss engulfed him was the softening sound of his heart beating away, even after all the years of inner torment and torture. His heart—it kept him alive, commanding him to remain.

But his mind, battled in return, saying, *Give up, you never had a chance.* In time, his mind defeated his heart, as minds often do, ripping him from consciousness. He drowned in the darkness, suddenly comforted by the realization that it was all over. There was no need to fight anymore.

There was no more fear.

He expelled one final breath, somewhere between a sigh of resignation and relief.

His mind accepted his fate.

But the heart was not so easily thwarted.

* * *

Growing up didn't ease my fears of the dark. In fact, as I got older, it scared me even more. As a child, the nightmares hiding in the dark are all in my head. They were scary stories fueled by nothing more than imagination. As an adult, I lived enough to know those scary stories are real.

A soothing rhythm found me within the deep darkness I awoke from. It was a dreamless sleep, a restless one. I heard the sounds first. Hushed whispers of voices I couldn't yet make out. Scribbling pens against paper. A faint pulsating static. My heart quickened, matching the rhythm which awoke me. I was convinced it finally happened. My sight was gone. I fluttered open my eyes and tested the other strengths of my body. My eyes remembered how to see, poorly, I admitted, but relief washed over me all the same. My time hadn't come yet. I let out a sigh, bringing my hands to my face to wash the panic away. Except, one hand stayed behind, resisted by an unknown force. Panic once again set in when a figure stood over me. Its muffled voice matched the blurry description of its face, both unknown and unrecognizable.

"Sir, my name is Officer Lance Stryker of the LVPD. You were in an accident. You're at Sunrise Medical Center. Sir, do you remember what happened?"

Words failed me as I tried to come to grips with what was happening around me. All I could remember was the desert, the car, Apollo, and . . . Tess. I stared up at the policeman with pleading eyes.

"Where is my wife?"

25

Interlude: Part 3

A man shoved at a duffle bag with a heavy push, cramming it into a space that, clear to all around him, was too small. He huffed raggedly, giving one more shove before turning his head in shame toward the stewardess holding a checked bag tag. He took his seat as though he was tempted to yell at the top of his lungs and kick the seat in front of him.

Marc watched the man for a moment, wondering if he'd finally break down if a stewardess informed him they were out of Diet Coke. The thought amused and relaxed him, if only for while. He turned to face the window playing over the script he'd written in his mind, trying not to second guess the reason he was on this plane in the first place.

That stubborn son-of-a-bitch had taken it too far this time. Las Vegas was tacky, hot and no place for a true artist like Killian. He had to know that, though Marc suspected reputation was one of the last things on Killian's mind. He had always been impulsive; some would even describe him as obsessive, but Marc knew that deep down Killian was as terrified as he was. He'd never admit that, though, especially to Killian. This had all grown much larger than some back-alley drug deal; lives were at stake, and Marc found confidence in knowing he was finally fighting for the good guys.

Admittedly, his tactics could use work. He wasn't too proud to admit that. The series of ominous letters he had sent Killian may have been a hair too threatening after careful reflection. If he thought too hard about it, he feared he may have been the one to push Killian right into the Empress's plans. Thankfully, Marc made a habit of not thinking too hard. His intentions were pure and that was what mattered. All he had wanted to do was protect his friend, the way he failed to protect him five years ago. No one could fault him for this, not even Killian St. James—emphasis on the Saint.

He didn't have much of a plan, aside from the obvious of flying to Las Vegas and saving Killian. The rest was unclear. There were still so many unanswered questions. What was waiting for him in Vegas? Would the man even listen to him? What exactly was Marc saving him from? That last one gnawed at him. He still knew so little of what the Empress was up to, but he knew in his gut that something wasn't right.

He'd had a momentary victory when he'd finally tracked down James Moore, resident drug dealer for the suspicious elite, but he still shuddered thinking about the wad of cash the man insisted on for passing along one of Marc's notes. Still, James was able to shed a small glimmer of light on the big picture, enough for Marc to confirm his suspicions. He had only ever a pawn in the Empress's master plan to get to Killian. Marc's ego was still recovering from that realization, but the phone number of the woman in 18C resting in his back pocket helped to ease his woes.

A wiser man may have spent the six-hour flight planning for the possibilities of what could go wrong, preparing for one of the most important conversations of his life. This man may have anticipated arriving at his destination only to find it bathed in disorienting, flashing lights. He would have been prepared for the reality that whatever it was he was here to do, he had arrived far too late. Thankfully, Marc was not a wise man.

"Sir, can I get you anything to drink today?" the stewardess asked.

"A rum and coke." Marc smiled his best smile. "And could you also, please, deliver a glass of bubbly to the woman in 18C?"

26

Without a Trace

We seek. Looking to find meaning in the night.
We pray. Waiting for an answer until we're sick and meek.
We lust. Hoping for guidance to come our way.
We learn. Living with a pain that never goes away.
We fight. Watching this torrid past burn.

Words have never been my forte. That was why I made my living as an artist. Art makes sense because it makes no sense. Art was created to express what words fall short in. I would create and imagine whole worlds out of nothing but lines, shapes, colors, and patterns—that had always been my escape. Now even my art mocked and tormented me. It held secrets and regrets, lies and heartache. I hadn't even had the courage to look at a paintbrush since she left, never mind pick one up. Still, painting would have been better than the endless pressure of shame for failing to find the right words. Words flip and tumble and somersault into different meanings. They take on new roles and portray new characters based on who controls the strings. Words can wrap around you tighter than the most comforting blanket, but words can also destroy you in ways that even they cannot describe.

She was the one who had a way with words. She could string pockets of sentences into moving speeches. The minute she spoke, anyone around her was helpless but to listen in awe. I am confident she could have moved a mountain if she sat down and talked with it for a while. Her words were the harmony of my life. They emboldened me and made me more than I ever could be alone. Her words were the only music I ever needed to listen to. Now the world was silent.

It had been three weeks to the day. Three weeks of silence.

Life had been a blur since I woke up in that hospital room. The doctors told me I had a concussion and two broken ribs. The police said my wife had left. They asked me if I knew where she had gone. My head was swimming for days, partly from the concussion, partly from the drugs, and partly because I could not and would not believe that Tess, *my Tess*, had left. They had no evidence, nothing to indicate that she had ever even existed. It was nearly a week before I was released from the hospital and when I returned home, I saw firsthand what the police had not seen.

I followed the footsteps of a previous life, the same path I had taken a mere six days earlier. I noted the lifeless kitchen, its glimmering steel and spotless marble. I trembled up the stairs, clutching the railing for support. When I reached the master bedroom, I was overwhelmed by the emptiness. There was nothing, not a pillow out of place, or a wrinkle to be seen. Before I even registered what I was seeing, my lips pulled and twisted against their will. They curved and stretched as a grave sob escaped their hold. Steaming tears fell one by one onto my cheeks and finally to the floor.

Six days ago I had stood right here, practically step for step, and listened to the woman I loved tell me she was carrying our child. In that moment, it was her that sobbed, not me. The bitter irony did not escape me. I fell to my knees, covering my eyes with the palms of my hands, trying to trap myself in those final few memories. That last beautifully tragic moment was now washed clean and replaced with the stark realization that Tess was simply gone. There was not a surface spared from the rampage of this reality. There were only faint rings of dust left where she once existed, the only whisper thin trace of her having ever been here at all. I thought about my own existence and if there would be any trace of me once I was gone. I wondered if I too would fade into nothingness. That's when I heard a knock at the door.

Of all the faces I could have conjured, Marc's was the last I expected. His hand was raised in a clenched fist, as if I had opened the door moments before he was going to knock again. His eyes were fixed on the ground, turning up in surprise when the breeze of the opening door crossed his face. He didn't speak, at first, but sadness filled his face. Finally, he said, "Killian, I am so sorry."

* * *

"It's peppermint," Marc said, handing me a steaming mug of tea. We still hadn't spoken much, but we were now sitting on the couches in the living room. Marc had taken immediate action, heading into the kitchen and brewing a pot of tea. I didn't even know I had tea, but Tess must have bought some before . . . The thought of her threatened tears back to the surface.

"I'm touched that you enjoy the tea that much, but no need for the waterworks." Marc chuckled wryly. He cupped his own mug, cradling it with both hands. I could see him working over the words he wanted to say in his head. On multiple occasions he almost said them aloud, but in the end, it was I who spoke first.

The words that fell from my lips surprised even me. They were kinder, gentler, than the years of words I had directed at him in my mind. His may not have been the friendly face I would have wished for, but in that moment I was only thankful not to be alone. "I think I'm ready to listen now," I said, "to whatever it is you've been trying to tell me. I'm ready."

"Ah, hmm," he murmured. Marc sighed and ran his fingers through his hair. He opened his mouth, then closed it again, he stopped himself several times before finally speaking.

He told me a story about meeting a woman at the bar and inviting her back to his apartment. He described how he experienced Apollo for the first time and the strange interest the woman took in me, of all things.

"I was there, that night at the showcase, to try to win back your friendship."

"What?" His heartfelt admission caught me off guard.

"After that woman showed me what Apollo could do, I knew it was only a matter of time before you found out about it. I realized far too late that you were the artist she was in town for. She was there to see you. I knew that if you had even an inkling of what Apollo was capable of, you'd never turn it down."

"Thanks for the vote of confidence, Marc," I scoffed.

"We both know it's not about that, Killian. I *know* you. You were my best friend. I wish I could turn back the clock and do things differently. I thought that was my chance."

"What do you mean?"

"Killian, I was there that night to stop you from trying Apollo. I was there to do what I should have done all those years ago; to keep you from making the same mistakes I had." Tears filled his eyes, but he quickly wiped them away before any could fall down his face. His confession was touching.

"You were a little late," I joked.

Marc's face fell even further, falling into his hands. His response filled me with guilt at my careless joking. I wasn't trying to deepen the cut. My years of rage toward Marc were difficult to let go, but he was here at the time I needed a friend most. I may have been too harsh on him.

"Marc, it's not your fault. That woman, her name is Pietra Perrault, and she was behind everything from the start. I'd been using Apollo for weeks before that showcase. Nothing you did or didn't do affected this outcome. Though you were right about one thing: I was hooked on that shit the second I tried it. How could I not be?"

Marc stood abruptly, pacing back and forth in front of his seat. "You don't understand. It *is* my fault! All of it. If I hadn't been a goddamn selfish, self-destructive addict when I met you, you wouldn't have fallen to my level. You never would have gone to rehab. You never would have been in this mess now. It's *all* my fault. I wish I could find a word better than sorry. It doesn't even scratch the surface of how I feel." He barely choked out the last few words through the sobs. "But Killian, I truly am so sorry."

He turned his back to me and continued crying, though growing quieter with each gasping sob. Seeing him in pain cut me like a knife. I'd spent so much time hating him that I never even considered he was in as much pain as I was. We both lost a friend back then, and I'd never considered how difficult that must have been for him. I found Tess, but for the past five years, Marc had been completely alone.

"Marc, it wasn't your fault then, and it isn't now. I blamed you once, but the truth is . . . " I was hesitant to admit what I'd ignored for a long time. "It was all me. I made those choices. You never forced the drugs on me. You may have led me to them, but it was my choice to use them. It was my choice to let it get out of control. Not to mention, if none of that ever happened, I never would have met Tess. So really, I should be thanking you."

I rose to meet him where he stood, still facing away from me. I laid a hand on his shoulder, trying to prove the weight of the words I was saying. "You were my best friend, and I let you take the blame for actions that were completely my own. For that, *I* am sorry."

Marc turned to face me; his eyes were bloodshot from tears he had furiously wiped away. His cheeks were red and puffy, and his bottom lip still trembled. He walked past me solemnly and sat back down in the love seat. He leaned back and ran his fingers through his hair once more before lacing his hands together atop his head and letting out a deep sigh.

I quickly understood his body language. I found my seat back on the couch, waiting for him to continue.

After a few moments of quiet, he continued. "When I arrived at the showcase, I saw that I was too late. Not only had you clearly already been using Apollo, but I found... Pietra, you said? Well, she was there too. She was watching you all night, tracking your every move."

Pietra had revealed herself nearly a week ago at the studio, but I was still grasping the full picture of her deception. Not only had she hired Jamie to target me, but apparently, she was stalking me too. I was trying to put together the pieces of her plan as Marc continued.

"Once I saw her there, I knew she was up to something. Of course, I couldn't know exactly what she had in mind, but I was determined to save you from whatever she had coming."

I completed his thought for him, "That's why you gave that threat."

"Yes. I thought if you believed someone was going to hurt Tess because of this drug, then you would stop. I know how much you loved her, Killian. I never would have hurt her. You have to know that. I never could have imagined . . ."

"She was kidnapped."

"What do you mean?"

"Tess didn't leave, not willingly. She wouldn't do that."

"But, Killian, there's no evidence of that."

"Exactly, Marc. There's no evidence of anything! The only thing I know to be true is that she's not here."

Marc sat speechless. I could see the wheels turning in his head, tactfully trying to plan his next words.

I filled in the words for him, "I believe she was kidnapped by Pietra Perrault."

"But why?"

"As collateral. Pietra brought me out to Las Vegas to create a collection of Apollo art for her, but she didn't know I had given it up. I met with her last week and refused to paint her collection. I don't think it's a coincidence that the same day I back out of our deal, my wife goes missing. Pietra kidnapped her. I know it. Better yet, I have proof."

I rose from my seat to head toward the bedroom and retrieved the notes I had received in New York. I climbed the stairs rapidly, bringing back flashes of childhood as I went running up the stairs at my parents' Hampton home. I wished for simpler times, when tripping up the stairs was the biggest excitement of my days.

When I came back down, I handed the box to Marc, eager to see his response. I knew what I had was incriminating evidence of Pietra's involvement in Tess's disappearance.

"Jesus Christ," Marc sighed. He took the notes out and held them tightly between his thumb and pointer finger, raising them above his head, "Killian, these aren't what you think they are."

"What are you talking about? Pietra sent me these threatening letters to scare me out of New York. It worked, obviously, but I didn't know it was her who sent them until a week ago. Look at that last one. *'Those you love will suffer.'* Marc, that's as obvious as it gets!"

"Killian, I sent these notes!" Marc shouted above my rambling.

The room went quiet. The blistering confession silenced every other sound in the world. My ears were ringing with confusion and denial.

"I sent the notes, Killian. After the showcase, I hoped my threat would stop you, but when I visited your office a few weeks later, I realized it wasn't enough. I sent the notes to scare you into sobriety. Pietra had nothing to do with it."

I was stuttering, barely stringing together comprehensible words. My head was pounding, and my vision spun out of control. "But, but she-she was behind it, she—You? But that means . . . "

I whispered my next words, not wanting to give life to the realization that was humming in my brain. If I said them aloud, then they had to be true. I wanted to save myself from their gravity, but they beckoned to be set free. "Tess left me."

Marc shook his head, despair spreading across his face. I found myself fixated by his hair swishing back and forth, an organic metronome keeping time with my throbbing heart. The rhythm lulled me into numbness. I was a blank slate, wiped clean by too much. Too much sadness, too much hope, too much disappointment. It was all too much.

This time, when the tears pushed against the iron gates of my heart, I let them out freely. They fell one after another until nothing but my shame remained.

27

Flight Risk

How do you take a chance in a world of doubt and betrayal?
I want to believe your hopeful words.
I want to achieve what my dreams have set forth.
I want to open myself to all the endless possibilities.
But I am afraid.

It was morning. Which morning, I was unsure. I didn't know how many days it had been, nor if it had been days at all. Had it been months? Years? Had I traveled back in time? I twisted to face the other side of the bed but found emptiness staring back at me. No, I was still trapped in the present, suffering through life without purpose. Tess was gone, this much I had come to terms with. I'd lost my love and my art. I had lost everything.

And yet, despite all I'd lost and the black void growing within my heart, I found friendship. Marc was a constant companion. He brought a steady supply of food and hot drinks. Sometimes he stayed and read snippets from the news, attempting to fill the dead air with something other than the obvious on both of our minds. I smelled cleaning chemicals at some point in my daze. I imagined him donning an apron and scrubbing every inch of the house like Cinderella. I understood his need to be doing something, to have a purpose. Mine was gone and I would have done anything to find it again, even cleaning the kitchen.

This morning was not unlike others I had experienced. The sun shone through the windowpanes, greeting the earth with its morning warmth. A fresh breeze filtered through the air. I thought Marc had opened a window downstairs before realizing that the open window was right in front of me. I stared past the empty side of the bed toward the sill. A bird landed on the windowsill. Flying in with a flurry of feathers and settling stoically as if it had never moved before. It looked at me. Staring right into my eyes. It was small, small enough to fit in the palm of my hand if I had the chance to hold it. There was nothing particularly special about it.

It perched there, wordless for a moment, surveying the world around it. Then, as if it found itself in distress at the sights it saw, it began to chirp uncontrollably. Such a mighty burst from such a small creature. It chirped until its little lungs ran out, calling out its song into a silent abyss. I wondered what the bird might be saying and who it was calling out to. I wondered if it was lost and searching for its way back home. As I stared back at the small bundle of feathers and beak, I became overwhelmed by emotion. I too was chirping into the abyss, waiting for an answer that would never come. I had strayed so far down the wrong path that I no longer knew how to turn back. The bird ceased its call and flew away, as quickly as it came. I shook my head, trying to break the trance that the small creature put me under.

Three years ago, I wouldn't have given that bird a second glance. I would be too busy on my way to some important meeting, yelling through my phone at a faceless investor. But Tess always loved the birds. I would wake up in the morning, cloaked in grogginess, and shuffle out to our balcony to find her silently basking in the sun. She would have a fresh cup of tea in her hands, listening to the orchestra of birds that accompanied the orchestra of city sounds. Her face would be lit by the subtle glow of the early morning sun; her legs curled up under her favorite knitted blanket. Tess was the only person I had ever known who could be perfectly content in the moment. Most people will never be lucky enough to experience true peace of mind even once in their lives. Tess made a living of it.

Sometimes I would catch her trying to hum along with the song of the bluebirds. A gentle smile danced across her face as they cooed and cawed in a melody I could never understand. Tess had a magical way of seeing the beauty in everything around her. She was her own kind of artist, painting her life the way she always dreamed, making beauty out of darkness in her own way.

As hard as I tried not to disturb the serene scene, she would always hear me behind her. She'd turn and stare at me with those beautiful eyes, warm and inviting, beckoning me to stay. "Come sit with me for a while," she'd say. She'd extend her hand as if to invite me into her little world of magic.

I rarely joined her. "Too much work to do, honey, I don't have time to listen to birds," I'd say. I'd retreat back inside and close the door on the birds and her.

It's the small things I regret the most. I wish I could have sat and listened with her. How foolish I was to let those moments go. I would give anything to go back and listen to the birds' songs with her. She was the thing that made this world beautiful. I wish I had been wise enough to see that before she was gone forever.

I rose from my living grave with a heavy sigh. Despite my best efforts, that little bird had inspired me. I wanted to soar high above my worries, weightless from guilt and sadness. I wasn't sure how I was going to get there, or if I ever would, but going down-stairs was a start.

Marc was sitting at the kitchen counter, hunched over a note-book. His brows were scrunched together in furious contemplation. His head was bent, devouring the pages of the book. His right hand held it flat, his middle finger supporting his current page, poised to push it aside at a moment's notice. His left hand framed his head, the pointer finger tracing the crease lines on his forehead.

"Must be a good book," I commented. "You look awfully invested in it."

I found a place at the counter next to him, peering over his shoulder at the object in his hands. The writing was handwritten, but moreover it was familiar. Its loops and swirls were ones I had seen time and time again.

"Marc, what is this?" I asked, the panic in my voice giving way to a slight tremble.

Marc closed the book and pushed it toward me. "I found it while I was cleaning up. It's from Tess, Killian. You need to read what is says."

28

Dear Killian

Why are the loudest voices the ones with least to say?
Why are the best moments the ones that never stay?
Where does the time go that was wasted away?

Where will my heart go once it's faded to gray?

"My story is one as old as time," I read.

I am sick. Not in body or mind, but in soul. I suffer from an illness that many before me have suffered. I am not unique in my suffering, but I am alone in this pain. My heart cries out to an empty audience, its plea heard by a jury made only of me. It aches and moans and yearns for a time in which it did not know suffering, a time before all of this. I am afflicted with the deadliest of diseases. It consumes my every thought, threatening to take hold of me wholly, letting loose on everyone and everything around me.

Mine is a pain that takes no prisoners. Any and all within my radius are victims to its fiendish schemes. It takes and destroys, leaving only victims in its wake. It has been known by many names, sometimes hiding behind its bolder, more tangible cousins, but that doesn't make it less dangerous. Guilt has no cure.

I used to think that the world was a decent place. In spite of the wars, famine and corruption, I believed in faith, karma and goodwill. Through each turmoil of my life, I found hope in my heart, even in my darkest moments. I never knew where this strength came from, but it was ingrained in me as deeply as the sequencing of my genes. It came to me when I needed it most and I welcomed it with open arms. I have never been forsaken by my beliefs, not until now.

I wanted to believe it's all been a terrible dream, a nightmare that I've yet to wake up from. I close my eyes and imagine my body, blissfully asleep in a warm bed, unknowing of the tragedy that has befallen this alternate self. As hard as I pray for that blissful version to be me, each dawn I am greeted with the same fate. The world suffered a terrible loss in the Fall. It will go down in history as one of the greatest catastrophes of civilization, I'm sure. A dark age for modern times. As much as I want to imagine the best in people, for the first time in my life I had doubts about what our future holds. The unknown is overwhelming. Its silence is deafening. It's enough to drive someone insane. That's another reality I hope for; insanity would be preferred to the truth.

I believed our marriage would never fail. *Til death do us part* sounded so definite in the moment. The stipulations were clear, the rules plainly spelled out. But what happens when death comes in a different form? There is no doubt that death visited us that night. It came in through the window maybe, or perhaps through the vents. It crawled along the floorboards, nary making a peep. It infiltrated our marriage bed and left shattered souls in its wake. I only wish it had visited us both.

That night brought the death of your dreams. All you had worked toward was swept away in the flood. Your sight, your true sight, was ripped from you. You lay there, peaceful and whole, sleeping right next to me, as you had done many nights before. We thought we were prepared. We knew the Fall would be a challenge, a hurdle for us to overcome, but I always anticipated doing it together. That's what we signed up for on our wedding day. We had fulfilled our vows of 'in sickness and in health' every day since we said them on that altar. I had no intention of letting the Fall stop that. We were a team, the best team, but then death parted us. Not in the traditional sense, but a part of you did die. I saw the spark drain from your soul the next morning when you opened your eyes and truly saw what had been taken from you. I was ready to join you in the land of the dead, broken but still together as one. We would trudge through the winding road of mourning hand in hand. But fate had other plans.

You lost your entire world, but I was spared. The Fall passed me over that morning and every morning since. Every blue-sky sunrise serves as a frightening reminder that my husband has gone to a place I cannot find. He has moved onto the next plane of existence, one of the masses of walking dead. I am condemned to stay behind, left woefully alone in the land of the living. A blessing that has cursed me to a life of *withouts*.

I'm haunted by a recurring dream where I visit our graves. Our tombstones sit side by side under the shade of a beautiful willow tree. A babbling brook sets the tone for remembrance and fond nostalgia. I'm bringing flowers, beautiful flowers full of bright vibrant colors, to leave at our graves. As I approach the plot, I read the epitaph engraved in our tombstones, etched forever as our legacy: Husband and wife, parted first by death, then by lies.

The flowers in my hands wilt and rot, turning gray before falling to pieces through my fingers. I wake in a sweat, the only proof I am still alive. Waking from a nightmare is typically a relief, but there is no comfort for me. I know that the dream is an awful prophecy I don't want to admit. This marriage is doomed to die a second time, which is why you could never know my secret.

Killian, you joined something unimaginable, that much is clear to me now. You crossed a line I thought you wouldn't dare come near again. That night at the gallery, I was surrounded by a sea of fire. Everywhere I turned, burning red eyes stared back at me. Chasing me. Mocking me. Finally, I sought solace in your eyes, ones I once knew better than my own. Your eyes had watched over me on sleepless nights and laughed with me in joyous days. But I don't know who that man was, chattering away with unholy creatures as if nothing was wrong in the slightest.

I was the only one in the room without those eyes. Did they know? I already pieced together what the blood eyes mean. You found a way to see color again. It's the only reasonable explanation for the change. You've been different, lighter, more hopeful. Your walk gentler, your touch softer. Your eyes were no longer darkened by what you had lost. Instead, they'd changed completely. I should have been appalled, or furious or terrified. Any of those emotions were right for this situation and yet, I felt proud. In spite of everything, I was proud of my husband. I still am.

Your paintings that night were inspired. I haven't seen you produce something so beautiful in years. Your usage of color was beyond imagination. You were inventive and whimsical while staying studious and solemn. You showed a depth to your soul few ever get to witness. A depth you used to share with only me.

It's clear I wasn't the only one taken by your eureka. I'd hardly seen the studio that busy since its opening. There was a buzz of wonder and discovery in the air. It was the same electricity I felt the day I first met you. Somehow, you managed to capture that and put it down on canvas for the world to see. You made true beauty out of collective sorrow. How could I not be proud of that?

The war inside my heart is one of constant pain and torture. My guilt weighs me down, dragging my feet along the ground. It tightens its grip on my lungs, squeezing the air out from under me. That night, I was afraid, but I could also breathe for the first time since the Fall. That night, I found hope. I can't fix what is broken. I can't remedy the injustice that fate brought to our lives, but I could protect what you found. You deserve to be happy, more than anyone I know. More than me.

But I still have so many questions. The logical thing to do would be to confront you, to find out the truth, but my heart is asking me to steady myself, to think before I act. The one thing I do know is that I haven't seen that spark in you since the night of the Fall. I haven't seen you smile as wide in months, and I know I would do anything to keep that smile on your face. I would even let you walk into fire.

A fresh start, at least on paper, is exactly what we needed. We needed to leave the past behind us, abandon the lies and the secrets and tragedies of the city. The ghosts of our past had no place in this new home, this new life. So, I said yes when you asked me to leave New York behind and fly to the desert. I was ready to find you again: my husband, the entrepreneur, the artist, my love. I wanted to relearn your ticks and rediscover your passions. I wanted to leave that unholy man behind, with his lies, his addiction, and desperation.

I knew that those were the dreams of a naive child, but I chose to believe them even still. A new location wouldn't change us back to who we used to be. A little sunshine cannot erase the hurt of the past. The body remembers, even when the mind wants to forget. That's the nature of trauma; it can never be fully erased. Trauma never goes away. It hibernates, waiting for the right time to strike, bringing you back into the darkness with it. I knew deep down that this move would not fix us. It would not change the guilt I have carried since your Fall. Nor would it change my withering trust each time you came home with scarlet eyes. It will not change your desire for success and the horrible lengths you will go to achieve it. Nor will it change the simple fact that I will never be enough for you. But I always hoped maybe, if I let you make this choice, maybe, you would love me as much as you love your art.

Killian, my darling, I know you love me. You have loved me since the day our eyes met. Even clouded by addiction, your heart knew my own in an instant. I have never been the same since that day, devoted to your embrace through thick and thin. I'm saddened to admit that since the Fall I have learned the harsh reality that I'd been spared from until now: Love is not enough.

I've been living in a fantasy, convinced that the love between us would conquer all. I was a child for believing it was that simple. The only way to ensure a brighter future is by working together, respecting each other and striving to create the lives we desire each and every day.

Once upon a time I had the faith we could do such things. I believed we could do anything, but now we are broken. We are holding on by a string, frayed at the core by secrets and lies. This new home cannot be built on a sinking foundation. We have come to a reckoning, and I don't know what the ending to our story will be anymore.

All I know is that despite what your words whisper to me. This move was not for us. I don't think it's even for you. We're running from it: your addiction. Its claws are latched deep into you once more. This monster has taken a new form, one I still don't understand, but its symptoms are the same. You can see it too; I know you do. I hear you calling for my help, desperate for me to save you again. I know that's why we left New York. It's your silent cry for help.

When my father got sick, I was helpless to stop him. I didn't know what to do, what to say or what measures to take. I was a child, lost in the complexities of addiction. I watched him dying slowly, day by day wasting away until we both knew the end was near. My years since in the clinic taught me the practical skills to handle addiction. I've helped countless others in ways I was never able to help my father, but now I'm that helpless little girl again.

Years apart and yet I am doomed to watch yet another man I love waste away. You are strong. You will not go as easily as he did, but you're not strong enough to do this alone and that is what breaks my heart. I am cursed with knowledge I thought would be my savior. I know what to do and yet I am frozen, unable to split my gaze between the man I love and the man who is a slave to his addiction.

I hear your cry, I hope you know that, and though you cannot hear me reply, I hope you see the love in my actions, the comfort in my trust. I cannot lead you back into the light until you ask me to and that eats away at me day after day. I'm sitting here, my hand in yours, watching you fall deeper down in darkness and knowing I am powerless to stop it.

This struggle is your own and only you can crawl your way back to the light. I hope you know that I'm here with you, for you, in every way I can be, but I cannot be *with* you anymore. I longed for the day when you were ready to tell me everything, when we could step closer together for the first time since we'd fallen apart. I swore on that day I would be there with open arms, ready to help you through anything, but things have changed now. It's not your life or mine anymore. Now there's her.

The air was heavy between us. Marc's eyes burn into me, pleading for resolution but not daring to speak it aloud. I thumbed through the remaining pages, looking up at Marc with wide, frightened eyes.

"There's only one more page," I whispered.

"We don't have to keep reading," he replied. "We can pick it back up tomorrow, or the next day. Whenever you're ready."

"No."

The thought of stopping was a voice I couldn't get out of my head. I wanted nothing more than to hold onto her forever, never turning the page to the ending of our story. Yet the truth beckoned, so I kept reading.

It was never my desire to have a child. I have never been gripped by the sight of a newborn babe or been enthralled with the laughter and cries of a toddler. I've never wished to impart my limited wisdom onto an offspring of my own. This is not the path I would have chosen for myself, and yet I lie here utterly enthralled by the realization that I will soon be a mother. I'm confused by my own reaction. My answer yesterday would have been unequivocally 'no,' but knowing what I know now, how can I say anything else other than 'yes?' I have never desired anything more; this child could not be more wanted, and I had hoped you'd feel the same.

In my dreams you hold my hand and tell me everything will be all right. You share your own secrets and vow to change. You fill me with promises and we are one again in the light of truth. You choose the right path. You choose us.

But when I heard that car pulling into the driveway and raced to the door it wasn't you I found. She was surrounded by a halo of light from the setting sun, but it was a trick. She was no angel. I wish I could say she was the devil, but that wouldn't be true either. She was simply a red-eyed messenger who had come to tell me the truth I had wanted for so long. My only wish was that it had come from your lips, not hers. Maybe that would have made a difference. Now, we'll never know.

I lowered the journal, hands trembling too much to continue reading the words before him. Tears stole what little clarity I had left in my vision. I dropped the booklet to the ground and covered my eyes with my fingers, enclosing myself in the darkness that consumed me from within.

Marc grasped my shoulder, squeezing firmly, before asking in a lowered voice, "Do you want me to finish it?" I nodded, stifling my sobs to hear Marc read aloud.

"Dear Killian, you know everything now and so do I. Our child deserves a life better than we're capable of creating together.

Maybe one day we can be a family again. Until then I promise to tell her stories of the man who painted magic from thin air. I promise I'll tell her everything, the good and the bad. I promise that I will reminisce on our time with fondness and not contempt. Most of all I promise that when I remember you, I'll remember you in red."

29

Cards on the Table

Righteousness is futile without courage.
Niceness is only betrayal without good.
Hopefulness is foolish without strength.
Wealth is only a mask without love.

The sun scorched the earth with unrelenting effort. The sidewalks steamed from the water trapped within them, erupting in gaseous fits. The soles of my shoes softened from the heated ground upon which they walked. It was barely April, yet Las Vegas was boiling.

I walked without purpose, aimlessly following Marc toward an unknown destination. He'd insisted on leaving the house. 'Getting some fresh air,' he called it. I knew what he was trying to do, of course. He was trying to distract me the best way he knew how. I trudged along, pretending to enjoy the not-so-fresh air as we continued our walk. I humored him because, despite the lack of success this outing was having, he was here and that mattered. I couldn't afford to push away any more friends.

"See, Killian, this is fun, right? Vegas, baby! It's like a city-themed amusement park for New Yorkers," he called out behind him.

"You bet, Marc."

"I promise you, Kel, this is going to do the trick. Wait until we get where we're going." He smiled.

My core ached from both regret and hunger, the two feeding on each other. I became aware of the sweat pooling on my lower back, undoubtedly leaving an unbecoming stain through my shirt. My pants chaffed at my legs and groin, forcing me to adjust with nearly every step. Though the physical discomfort was growing, I tried to push it from my mind for Marc's sake.

We passed scores of people. Throngs of tourists and streams of natives trying to dance around each other in a game of rhythmic chess. The sight made me homesick, longing for the simplicity of the city. In New York, this game would be over quickly. There would be no dance, no strategy. The determined would split through the aimless without second thoughts. It was brutal, but direct. It left no room for misinterpretation or option for failure. It was dog eat dog, but at least you knew where you stood. Here, I was lost in every way I could be.

A blast of cold air drew my attention. It was followed almost immediately by the overpowering smell of cigarettes. It was comforting in the way that a library was comforting, warm with nostalgia and rife with possibilities. I followed the breeze and the smell to set my sights on a street level casino. It wasn't one of the fancy ones attached to the upscale hotels that lined the Vegas strip, but it was still full of patrons in the middle of the afternoon.

"Ta-da!" Marc exclaimed, extending his arms toward the casino.

"This is it?" I replied, trying to match my tone to curiosity rather than a sneer.

"That it is. Come on, let's go blow off some steam."

I followed him through the sliding doors. For the first time since leaving home, I felt a rush of anonymity. This was a place that drew everyone's gaze away from you. Hope was on the line, and it deserved far more attention than even a scantily clad showgirl. I could be a no one here, melting into the walls. I couldn't believe Marc was right. It was intoxicating.

I found a seat in front of a slot machine. It was an old one, with a lever still initiating the spin instead of a button. It didn't have the lights or the whistle of a newer machine, but I suspected I had the same a chance of winning a fortune. I dug a few quarters out of my wallet and slid them into the machine, pulling the lever with cautious optimism. As the wheels spun before my eyes, I wondered why they ever changed the machines. Pulling a lever would always be far more exciting than pushing a button. One by one, the wheels jutted to a stop, revealing my winnings—nothing.

I absentmindedly laughed aloud before darting my eyes across the room to see if anyone had heard me. There was a middle-aged woman in the chair next to mine. She was smoking a cigarette, and on her machine rested an ashtray that held at least a day's worth of remains. She stared straight ahead, eyes glazed over as she pulled the slot lever over and over again, hardly even noticing the results. If she did hear my outburst, she paid no mind.

"Ah man, those penny slots never pay out," Marc had returned and was hovering over my shoulder as I pulled the lever down again.

"I don't know what era you're living in, but you can't get anything for a penny in this place." I chuckled.

"Yeah, yeah. Either way, you need to try your hand at a real game. How about some roulette?"

We approached the table and witnessed the tail end of the current round. The scene was taught. There was a collective experience of anticipation radiating from the small spinning ball. The ball slid around and around, skipping rapidly from slot to slot until suddenly it found its home. Half the table sighed. Dejected mumbles rumbled through the defeated group. Simultaneously, the winning side cheered in hush whispers, restrained by courtesy and ego. The sight brought a smirk to my face. It was comforting to know that after so much had changed, some things remained constant. My world was turned upside down, but casinos still reeked of smoke and red always wins.

Except that wasn't true at all. I walked slowly toward the table in shock, forcibly pushing past several displeased onlookers. I peered at the wheel, primed for its next showing, and braced against the edge of the table as realization sank in. At first glance, I hadn't noticed the subtle, but profound changes to the game. Now it was boring into my eyes with a fury that could only be from cosmic malice. Black and red were no longer sworn enemies. Red was gone, replaced by white. I swung my head on a swivel, realizing what I had missed in my time on the casino floor. All colors had already been replaced. Every game was being played in black and white. There wasn't a muddy gray swatch to be found. There was no way to tell that another color had ever existed here at all.

Red wasn't the only victim. I saw a tray of chips go by on a waiter's tray. The chips were now shaped according to their amount. The circular outline remained, now enhanced by differing levels of height, respectfully increasing. A shallow ring was engraved on the side for a tactile indication of the chip's value. It was innovation in action, an ingenious solution to a problem once solved by color.

It shouldn't have shocked me. It was only a matter of time before the world found a way to move on from color. Too many critical layers of infrastructure were based on color. New solutions would have to be made and made quickly. All of this raced through my rational brain at a speed barely shy of the dark thoughts that won the race.

How could everyone move on so easily? There wasn't a patron in the hotel that appeared the slightest bit bothered by the new developments. I heard no chiding women discussing the changes over cocktails. There was no fumbling dealer who had to correct himself from calling something by its color. No one seemed affected by the changes at all. No one except me.

My heart sank to the pits of my stomach. What had it all been for? Everything Apollo took from me—for what? For a world that didn't even care. I pushed back from the inner circle of the next roulette game. I hurried away from the dealer announcing bets on black versus white. I reached where Marc was standing, leaving a wake of glares from people I had shoved past.

"Killian, hey! Pretty sweet, huh? Nothing is better for the soul than some recreational gambling, huh?"

"I'm going to go get some air," I replied, trying not to show how uncomfortable I was. I needed to escape this scene quickly.

"Oh, let me come with you."

"No need." I faked a smile. "I'll come back and meet you here. I need a quick breather."

I was already walking away before Marc could reply. I walked toward the shining light of the doors that exited back onto the main strip sidewalk. I slowed slightly as I walked past the slot machine I had, only moments ago, found my first moments of levity from. Now that laughter was a distant memory.

I caught sight of the bar before I reached the exit and felt that familiar tug of sickly hope. This was not the same hope that leaves schoolgirls dewy eyed and sighing at the quarterback. This hope steals away into your mind, sewing dangerous seeds.

I took a seat on a bar stool toward the end of the counter. The mirrored bar reflected back at me, forcing me to come face-to-face with a man I no longer recognized. The face that stared back at me was one of a man who had made all the wrong choices and learned no lessons from his folly. He had been the cause of his own demise and still had the audacity to mope about it. I averted my eyes from the sulking sod in my reflection to scan the selections of alcohol featured on the back wall. I'd fallen off the wagon months ago, but I supposed it was as good a time as any to abandon it completely.

"Hey kid, what do you have to be day drinking about?"

I turned to face the man who called out to me from the seat a few down from mine. He was an older man, close to his mid-sixties. His hair was thinning and had receded far down his scalp, but he hid it with a straw cowboy hat. Despite showing its age up top, his hair flowed gently over his shoulders, falling in a silver waterfall down his back. His shirt was tie-dyed, a conglomerate mess of grays in current sight. He wore faded denim jeans and flip-flops to complete the ensemble. He was a relic from a bygone era, not unlike myself.

"I'm sorry about your shirt," I replied.

"What about it?" the man called back, glancing down at the garment.

"I'm sure it was quite a sight before . . . " I trailed off, "Everything was beautiful back then."

"Ah Hell, son, that moping has got to quit."

"But don't you miss it?" I met his eyes, willing him to answer honestly, to understand my pain and prove I wasn't alone in desperation. I needed him to justify my actions. It was a tall order for a stranger in a casino bar.

"Sure." He shrugged, bringing a sigh of silent relief from my end of the bar. "But there are a lot of things I miss."

I furrowed my brow, waiting for him to go on.

"I miss when bell-bottom jeans were in style. I miss jukebox school dances. I miss my wife." He stared at his drink. Maybe he was trying to find his own answers in it, or the strength to keep going, "but I don't let that stop me from living my life. The past ain't a good place to set up shop. You've got to move on. That's the only way to survive."

I knew what he said was true. I believed it more than anything. But I also knew that the future was not something I wanted to be a part of. I didn't deserve to find happiness again. Any misery or hopelessness I experienced from this day forward was of my own design. There was no place for me in this changing world. I should do it the favor of not saving a spot in line.

I reached into my pocket and pulled out my last Apollo roll. I'd been saving it for a special occasion. None of that mattered anymore. I lit the tip and sucked in the bittersweet fumes.

"Thank you for your advice, sir. I think I'm going to take it."

I rose from my stool, abandoning the drink I never ordered and walked straight for the door. I took another hit of Apollo as the steam of the air hit my face and the sun flashed into my sight. I turned out of the building and walked down a familiar path, back to the life I deserved, back to my self-made destruction and back to her. Pietra's deal was the bed I had made and now I was ready to lie in it.

30

Seeing Red

I am her, but she is not me. We're woven together like rings of a tree.
But I am not her because she is me.

Colors cascaded around me. Scarlet, crimson and ruby fell in droplets across the floor. Their vibrancy contrasted with the stark paleness of the concrete floors. Gravitational drops, large and small, littered the area where I stood, painting a timeline of indecision. They fell from my sopping brush, soaked by the fury of my painting. I was lost in the emotion of my work. I painted with little care or delicacy. My former methods of control and precision were gone, overtaken by a burning need to put my soul on the canvas.

Anticipation, hopefulness, insecurity, shame—these were children's feelings. Now I knew what true emotion was. It ate away at my dignity, my will to live. My every thought was consumed from within. I was blind in the darkness of its overwhelming control. I feared I would succumb, drowning in the abyss, if I didn't expel it. So, I painted.

I didn't know how long I'd been in that studio. I recognized the passing of time only by the way the light moved around me, inspecting me from every angle. Oh, what the sun must be seeing. A man with uncontrollable emotions, desperately trying to process his thoughts through art. He paced the room, aggravated by the result of his work. He wished to be rid of his torment but found himself surrounded by her face.

Tess's face stared back at me from every corner of the room. Her beauty mocked me, tormented me. I came here to dispel her from my mind and yet she was the only thing I could paint. I painted her over and over again. The studio was littered with canvases, all marked with her face.

The eyes are the purest part of our bodies. They hold our truths and our secrets. They are the gateway to love and wisdom. Her eyes were seared into my head, never allowing me to forget them, and yet I could not paint them. The eyes I remember belonged to my wife, the woman I loved. That woman was dead. The face that stared back at me now was one of a person I never knew. She was a version of Tess that existed outside my knowledge of her. I think that was why I couldn't paint her eyes. I never knew who she truly was.

I wiped a bead of sweat from my brow, leaving a streak of paint in its place. I was exhausted, drained from the exertion of not only painting, but of processing my trauma. The chaos inside had been released, left for dead on the canvases before me. Now I was finally free. I took another hit from the joint resting on my easel. My vision throbbed as more colors joined the solemn party. My eyes burned, burdened by too much too fast. I knew this was accelerating the blindness, but I didn't care anymore. I had nothing left in the world I wanted to see. I was finishing off the joint as the door behind me clicked open. I heard a pair of heels pacing closer, hands of a clock keeping time, before stopping abruptly. I'd been expecting her.

"Should I add breaking and entering to your list of offenses? Right next to breach of contract?" Her arms were crossed, and her lips pressed into a straight line. I could see right through her facade. She was relieved to see me.

"Can it, Pietra. It's not B&E if you gave me a key." I whipped the key out of my pocket and flung it toward her. It skittered along the floor, traveling with a tinkling tone. Pietra's pointed shoe rose and stopped it in its tracks.

"All right, Killian, I'll bite. What is this?"

"This? This is my end of our bargain. You're welcome." I gestured around me at the multitudes of canvases around the studio. "I think it's some of my *finest* work, and I think you'll see it meets all the qualifications." I gave a subtle bow, holding the smoking Apollo high above my head to seal in the words.

Pietra walked closer, examining my series. As she approached, I saw more clearly what I hadn't from a distance. Her hair, usually sleek and straight, was stringy, as if she hadn't washed it in days. Beyond that, she wore dark circles under her eyes. Her complexion was rough and red. Behind her gold-rimmed glasses bloodshot eyes matched her red irises. Together it appeared as though her eyes were slowly filling with blood. She was using too much, and it was showing. After finding out how she manipulated me, I thought I would be glad to see her struggling, but it brought me no joy. I felt only pity when I looked at her.

"This is truly your best work, Killian. The exhibition will be a knockout. Will your wife be in attendance again?" I knowing smile crept up her face.

"No, my wife is dead." I replied, turning to walk out the door.

Pietra called after me, "You're leaving? After all that?"

I stopped walking but didn't turn back to face her with my reply. "I've fulfilled your contract. We're done here."

She scoffed, "Like husband, like wife."

Her words stopped me in my tracks. "What did you say?" The question came out as almost a snarl.

I turned to face her as she spoke, her voice rising with the same indignation as a teacher in a rowdy classroom. "I said, 'like husband. like wife!' The both of you, running from your challenges. Once I told her the truth of what you've been doing, the reason you dragged her to this godforsaken desert, she ran from what she couldn't face. I thought you were stronger than she was, but even I can be wrong sometimes. You two really were made for each other."

I knew she was trying to get a rise out of me, egging me on with her admission. It might have worked too, had Tess not gotten the better of us both first. Even still, dark thoughts flashed in my mind. I saw myself wringing her neck, snuffing out her life like she snuffed out mine. She ruined my life for little more than greed, yet even as my hands reached out, they did not go for her throat. I held her face in my hands for only a brief second before crashing into her, my lips meeting hers with a jolt of force. All my rage and need for revenge manifested into one smothering kiss. I couldn't explain what brought on this reaction. Conscious thought had left my mind, leaving behind only carnal instinct.

I pulled away long enough for the shock to register in both of our eyes, but not before she pulled me in, kissing me back. Our hands fumbled, blindly ripping away at the other's clothing. We bumped into walls and stumbled further into the gallery. We pushed through a door and landed on something soft. There was only the sound of her breath, heavy with mine and the warmth of her hands on my skin.

My mind left my body, hibernating in some safe place where there was only me and Tess, happy and together, hidden from the reality of this room.

31

Take My Hand

It feels so nice
Is that not reason enough?

It feels so real
But it will never be enough.

The sun seeped in through the curtain-less gallery windows, filling the room with a pale, hazy glow. Close to setting, it was stealing away the clarity of the daylight, leaving only ambiguity and shadows for the poor souls who dared to traverse the nightscape. I surveyed the surrounding room, taking stock of my surroundings for the first time. In the haste of the moment, I hadn't taken any notice of where I'd wound up.

I was in a storeroom at the back of Pietra's gallery. Shelves of utility equipment lined the walls, waiting for a moment to prove their worth, a moment that may never come again. There was a single fluorescent light over my head, but it was dark for now. I imagined it would fill the room with a sickly, stark light once the sun finally set. For now, I enjoyed the subtle rays of lingering daylight that filtered in from the small egress windows lining the top of the room. I lay on a mattress, propped up by wood pallets in the middle of the floor. The sheets were soft and silken, indicating they once lined a bed of far more luxurious status than this paltry storeroom cot. To my surprise, the bed was not uncomfortable, despite its poor appearance.

Realization struck me as I glanced at a pale, delicate figure beside me. Her back was turned toward me, hiding her face as she burrowed into the sheets. She was living here. More evidence piled up as I saw a suitcase and its contents littering the floor. Bags of makeup, jewelry and travel toiletries sat in line along with the gallery equipment. A small vanity mirror had been placed upon a cardboard box. The scene was becoming more and more clear as I turned in each direction, unfolding before my eyes.

Pity, vindication, disgust or shame would have been appropriate for the moment, and yet I felt nothing. Not a twinge of anything more than complete indifference. There was too much sorrow, too much regret and too much heartbreak for anything else at all to crawl to the surface, even for her.

She rolled over gently, facing me for the first time since we finished. She said nothing, but I saw in her eyes the words she contemplated saying. She didn't need to speak for me to know what she would say. Her eyes glistened with tears that would never fall. She was too strong for that, even now. Her harsh exterior had been stripped away, her secrets laid bare. Still, she would not cry, not in front of me, and for that, I was surprised to find, I respected her immensely.

"It was never about you," she finally said. Her voice was quiet, but strong. It didn't quiver with vulnerability or hide in a whisper.

"I know," I replied.

She rose from the mattress, walking evenly toward the suitcase in the corner and the pile of clothes rising from inside. I took a moment to watch her, taking in the sight of her body that I hadn't cared to notice during our fit of passionless sex. I had once revered her as a mythical creature, slender and alluring, but in this light, she was no more enchanting than any other woman. I could see now that her slenderness came from lack of nourishment. There had been too many sleepless nights, too many forgotten dinners and too few meals prepared with anything other than disgruntled haste. Her skin had dulled, and her eyes were sunken back more than I recalled. She was a shell of her former self. The image made all the more apparent by the over-sized T-shirt she donned before coming back to the mattress. She sat upright, her posture taught and refined. She held her head high despite the cracks in her appearance she knew I could see.

"We're not nearly as different as you might believe," she said softly, "the only difference is that you had her." Her head hung low, the first sign of self-pity dancing across her face before she regained her composure. "You, of all people, should understand. I couldn't start over again. I've worked too hard to have it all ripped away. You have to understand."

I did, of course. More than anyone else ever could.

"I did what I needed to stay afloat, but even all that couldn't keep the lights on. This gallery is everything. It's my life's work, my sole showing of my time on this earth. When it became clear that I could either keep my apartment, or the gallery..." She gestured to the room around us. "The choice was easy. You were my last hope, Killian. Apollo was an awakening, but my gifts lie in curating fine art, not creating it. I needed—" She stopped herself. "I *need* you."

Her words weighed heavy with sincerity. They resonated with a core pillar of myself that I didn't want to give voice to. I knew her.

I understood her. I was her, or I could have been had it not been for . . .

"But I needed her," I filled in.

She nodded, confirming the unspoken parallels between us.

"I never wanted to be the villain of your story. I hope you know that, but I had to do what was necessary. I had to take care of myself. I don't have the luxury of someone else caring for me." That mask was back again. The one she wore to hide her emotions, the raw strength and resilience, with uncompromising belief in herself. But her confidence faded after her own words sank back in. "For what it's worth, I'm sorry for the part I played in it."

The 'it' she referred to was undoubtedly the collapse of my marriage, my relapse, and the downfall of my life as I knew it. There was a lot of baggage packed into that one little 'it.' She was an easy outlet to blame. On the surface, she was the driving force for all that had gone wrong in my life over the last six months. But I knew that wasn't fair or true.

"Whatever part you played; my actions were mine alone. This blame is mine to carry." I held her stare, hoping she would take to heart the words I was saying. Marc had shown me that guilt was a heavy load to bear, especially when it's not your own. I wasn't willing to let her take the fall for this. I could not make that mistake again.

Her face lit up, freed from the weight of holding back the truth. I finally saw her for who she was, a reflection of myself. She was the manifestation of loneliness and isolation. She was a woman driven by her passions and fiercely loyal to her career. She was someone who had been pulled in too deep and had no lifeline to reel her back.

"I'm afraid to start over," she whispered, the confidence in her voice faded. "I don't know if I have the strength anymore."

Her fears were my own. They were the fears that led me to Apollo in the first place. I didn't know if I had the strength either, or the will to even try. I reached out and squeezed her hand. It was a small gesture, one that could be interpreted in any multitudes of ways. I couldn't pretend to have the answers. I wouldn't do us both the disservice of delivering any final platitudes. Our story was complete. We were free now, with only the future to face, and for that I would always be grateful.

"Goodbye, Pietra."

I collected my things and strode out of the gallery, leaving her and that chapter of my life behind.

* * *

"Killian! Where the hell did you go?" Marc's voice sprang from my phone. "You left to 'go get some air' six hours ago, man."

"I know, I'm sorry. I shouldn't have abandoned you, but listen, I'm standing outside this burger joint near the giant Ferris Wheel. I don't know about you but—"

"I'll be there in five," he said as he hung up the phone.

I chuckled and soaked in the simplicity of the moment. It had been far too long since I had a good burger with a friend. I watched the street, expecting to see Marc breathlessly rounding the corner any second. He'd race down the restaurant lined corridor, not even mentioning my sudden disappearance. He'd make some joke about it, and we'd laugh and leave it all behind us. I knew without a doubt what my future held for the next ten minutes. Beyond that was a mystery, one yet to be written, but at least it was mine. The roar of the Vegas strip was nearly deafening. Casinos clattered and tourists chattered, and music played far too loud, but the silence of clarity shielded me from its overwhelming force. I was in control of my future. I always had been, but this time I was ready to take the reins. I wanted to believe I wouldn't make the same mistakes, push away the same good people, or choose the same wrong roads to take. But the truth was that I didn't know. Maybe I was destined to repeat my past, to succumb to my shortcomings again and again.

I saw Marc appear at the far end of the corridor, waving me down and beginning the series of events that had played out in my mind. The one thing I did know was that no matter what the future held, I wanted more moments like this one.

32

The Spring

Your words warm me. Your touch tempts me.
Your heart beckons me. Your mind inspires me.
Your eyes see through me. Your kiss revives me.

You are the sun.
But I am the moon you couldn't be further from.

"Are you ready for this?" Marc watched me with careful eyes from the seat next to mine.

Passengers filed onto the plane in organized chaos. A baby screamed in the back row as frustrated socialites rolled their eyes and whispered to one another. Young backpackers attempted to shove their over-sized hiking bags into the minuscule space under their seats. A flight attendant kindly told a frantic man that his roller bag was too large and must be checked.

Life in all its chaotic glory continued around me, oblivious to the disasters I'd experienced. I sat there, baffled how no one could realize that my world had fallen apart, when it dawned on me how many others had sat exactly where I was sitting. How many people had sat on this plane as their world was flipped upside down? How many people had I walked past, oblivious to a pain all too obvious to them?

"As ready as I'll ever be."

We were on a plane back to New York, Marc and me. There was nothing left for me in Vegas. It was only ever meant to be a temporary home. In truth, it was never a home at all. I wanted to blame the sun and curse the sand for all the awful memories stuck inside my head. I wanted to hate this city, but I didn't. It never did anything to me. Places don't cause disasters. Cities don't harbor memories. People do, and the person who caused all those awful memories left, bringing disaster home with him.

"I'm glad you're here, Marc. Thank you for coming to get me."

"You don't need to thank me, Killian. That's what friends do. That's what I should have done all those years ago. I let you down then, but I won't this time. You'll get through this, and I'll be there for you along the way."

I smiled gently. Marc was a good friend. I was glad to have him back by my side.

"Should we head right to your studio when we get back?"

"No, not yet. First, I need to settle some unfinished business."

* * *

After leaving Pietra, I thought I would be free of any lingering ribbons of the past, but I was still haunted by one loose thread. It filled my dreams, begging for its call to be answered. For years I had shoved it aside, focusing on more important things, but it was always there, biding its time. In the quiet of that empty house, it finally crept to the surface. It filled my chest and threatened to come bursting from my throat. I had no chance of a happy future until I was free from its hold. Strange how after six hours stuck on a plane I finally found the courage to confront it. It was time to finally put the spirits to rest.

My father's grave lay under a grand tree. What variety of tree eluded me, but the tree was as stately as my father would have expected. Its trunk expanded outward enough I couldn't wrap my arms around it. The thick branches allowed almost no sunlight to shine on his tombstone, even in winter when all the leaves had fallen. The permanent shadow was fitting for him. He was not a man who ever craved the sun, though he did love a spotlight. He wasn't a man who concerned himself with pitiful things, such as fair weather or a nice view. He was a man of action who had forged his own path in life.

What my father accomplished in his lifetime was impressive. Many had spoken of his legacy even after he was gone. My father was not loved by many people, but he was respected by all, and that's how he preferred it. That's what happens to a person who's had to work too hard for all they have. They're hardened by their experience, jealous of all those around them who walked an easier path. My father was an envious man, and he wanted to be envied as much as he envied others. It was a toxic cycle that consumed his waking hours.

He met my mother when she was nineteen. He was twenty-eight at the time, causing a stir in the crowds he socialized with. She was beautiful, a classic beauty the great twentieth century authors would have written about. Her skin was fair, never tarnished by a blemish in her life. Her cheeks were naturally rosy, touched by the faintest bit of rouge when she was trying to look particularly glamorous. Her blonde hair held a gentle wave that effortlessly fell around her shoulders. She kept her hair long and meticulously styled. She loved trying new and innovative fashions with her hair.

The experimentation was always her aim, not the outcome. I believe that's where my creativity came from. It brings me peace to know that a part of her lives within me each time I pick up a brush.

Conversely, it always brought me smug satisfaction to know I was provoking my father's spirit each time one of my paintings sold. My father was not a kind man. Stern, proud, and fair were words to describe him. Never warm, loving, or nurturing. He wanted me to follow in his footsteps and become a stockbroker. He had tall dreams for me, even when I was a child.

Academic excellence was never enough for him. Absolute perfection was what he demanded. He wanted the best, and that included me. His standards were too high. I was in first grade when I earned my first low mark. When he found out, my father bellowed in a way I had never heard before. He was a crazed animal, barking and howling until his mouth foamed. He smashed toy trains against the wall and launched fluffy teddy bears out my bedroom window. I was locked in my room for a whole day with no food.

I decided then and there that I would no longer play his game. Only seven years old and already a rebel. I learned to endure his punishments, which only came more frequently as my grades constantly floundered below the level of perfection. I hid a pack of crayons and a stack of paper under my bed for the days I was locked inside. Sitting on the floor of my bedroom, tear marks staining my cheeks and hunger rumbling through my stomach, I became an artist. In a way, I should be grateful for his severe reactions. I might not have become the man I am today without them. In fact, I'm certain I would not have.

"Hi, Dad." I brushed away some leaves from his grave marker, tracing the inscription carved into the stone.

Father and son. May his legacy live on forever.

I wasn't sure who picked it out for him, but he would have approved.

"It's been a while, hasn't it? God, it's been over twenty years. I bet it pisses you off that I don't come to see you more, huh?" I chuckled at the thought. All of heaven to revel in and my father would be concerned with how often his son visits his grave.

"Well, I'm here now. The prodigal son returns! I bet you're happy with how I've turned out. I bet you're fucking tickled that my life is such a mess. You never wanted me to be happy. You only wanted me to be some plaything that you could brag about to your stupid drinking buddies. Another perfect porcelain figurine. Same as mom." I turned toward my mother's grave. She lay a mere few feet away, poetically bathed in sunlight. I loved my mother, but she was not innocent.

I found myself speaking to her now. "Why didn't you ever do anything to stop him? How could you let him treat me that way? You let that monster lock your own son away. You did nothing!

"I'm glad you both died." Tears stung my face as the admission left my lips in a whisper.

"I said it. I'm glad you're both dead. I think it's the best thing that ever happened to me. You want to know why? Because if you hadn't died then I would have ended up just like you. The both of you."

"If that's selfish of me to say then I accept it. I'll take being self-ish over being a carbon cut-out copy any day. I'm proud of who I am. I'm proud of the choices I've made, even the bad ones. I'm an addict, but I'm also an artist. A successful one, I might add. I did what everyone dreams of. People buy my art. They love it! You hear that, Dad? They love me!

"But you know what's the real kicker? I did it all to spite you. I knew with each painting I made, every brushstroke, you were rolling in your grave. I loved it. When that wasn't enough, I rolled joints and snorted lines. I spent every waking hour trying to come up with new ways to torment you. All this time I thought I was trying to prove myself to the world, to the critics, to my wife, but it was always you. You died over twenty years ago and yet you still have as strong a hold on me now as you did then. Not anymore. I'm through with living in your shadow. I'm done trying to prove my worth to a ghost. You can't haunt me anymore. I won't let you."

I stood shakily, my knees buckling under the weight of my admissions, and walked toward the cemetery's entrance. I took one step, then another, walking away from the grand tree and my parents' gravestones. I knew I'd never return to this place, at least not in this lifetime. I forced myself not to turn back, focusing only on each small step forward.

33

Epilogue

Two Years Later

What you didn't know was that I wanted you too.
And what you don't know is that I still do.

Petal rested her head on my shoe. She huffed a great sigh as she relaxed against my loafers. Evidently Seth's graduation ceremony was far from interesting for dogs.

"Tough day for you two? It's only one in the afternoon and Petal can barely stay awake!" Marc sat back down in the seat next to mine, placing a bottle of water in my hands.

"She's saving her energy," I said, bending down to scratch Petal behind the ears, "she knows we're going to the P-A-R-K after this." One of Petal's droopy ears perked up at the sounding out of letters to her favorite place. She was too smart for her own good.

"If this thing ever gets going." Marc munched impatiently on popcorn. It was true, it had been nearly thirty minutes since we sat down in the auditorium. There was a dull hum reverberating throughout the theater as people made small talk, waiting for their graduate to arrive.

"What's Seth's last name again?"

"It's Abbott."

"Thank God, he's an 'A,' that means we get to duck out of here early."

"What's the big rush, Marc? Can't you relax for a minute and smell the roses?"

"The only rose I smell is the undeniable perfume of too many people inside on a hot New York summer day. Jesus, Kel, ever since you went blind, you're such a hippie."

We both laughed. He wasn't far from the truth. I'd had a reawakening since losing my sight. The world was dark and yet everything seemed so clear. Time moved slower, flowers smelled sweeter, and grass felt softer. I was happier, or at least as happy as I could be.

In the nick of time "Pomp and Circumstance" played through the loudspeakers. Marc let out an exaggerated sigh, mumbling, "Finally!" through a mouth full of popcorn. I chuckled and readied myself for when Seth's name was called.

As I listened to the orator giving her invocation, I found my mind drifting back to the day I asked Seth to take over the studio. It had been nearly two years since that day, but I remembered it perfectly.

"The place looks great, Seth."

I was enjoying the surreal experience of being given a tour of my own studio. I'd only been gone for a few weeks, but Seth had been working diligently to revitalize the gallery. A multimedia display sat front and center in the open room. Ceramics, sculptures, metalworking, oil painting, and watercolors lived side by side in joyous harmony.

"Once you left, we needed more work to fill the space. I opened it up to submissions from the community. There are some really talented people out there, Boss—I mean, Killian. Sorry, I'm still getting used to that one."

I smiled warmly. I hadn't stopped smiling since I entered the gallery. Its familiar sights and smells brought me back to a happier time.

"I love your ideas, Seth. This is great."

"I haven't even mentioned the best part!"

"Oh?"

"These last few weeks have brought in more money than all our Apollo showcases combined. You should have seen the turnout for the last open gallery night. It was packed in here! I guess people need a sense of community right now."

"I'm glad we can be rid of Apollo. It wasn't good for us." That was perhaps the biggest understatement I could have made.

Apollo was all that remained of a world gone by. Generations from now children will only know the world as it is: gray and monochrome. Apollo would pass, as all great fads do. It would die out with those who still remember the world before the Fall. It was time for a new generation to take control. One that could move on from the past and pave the way for the future. It was Seth who had brought sustainable change to this studio. He was the future. I was sure of it.

"Seth, we need to talk."

"Oh right, of course, I knew this was coming. You're back now, so you'll be taking over again, right? I mean, it only makes sense."

He was too humble for his own good, never realizing when I was trying to give him a compliment.

"That's not what I was going to say."

Surprise lit up his face as quickly as confusion darkened it. I had to admit; I was enjoying the suspense. Seth was the little brother I never had. Teasing him could rival any comedy special for good entertainment.

"Seth, I've known since you came to work here that you had a bright future ahead of you. You've only proven yourself time and time again. You followed me right into the line of fire and never even blinked. I can never repay you for your friendship. It was clear to me when I left you in charge that you were the future of this studio, not me. I'm even more confident in my decision after seeing what you've done these past few weeks."

"What are you saying?"

"I'm saying that I want you to take over the studio. Permanently. You can finish your degree, of course, and I'll still be around to help if you need it, but . . . "

"But?"

"But it's yours, all of it. If you want it."

"There's no if's about it, Killian. I want it." Seth clasped my hand in his and shook vigorously. He wore a schoolboy grin that half convinced me he was fifteen again. His feet could barely maintain their positions, bobbing up and down in a march of silent celebration.

I heard Seth's name called and Marc letting out a joyous *whoop whoop* beside me. Even Petal let out a small chirp in congratulations. I joined in with a holler of my own amid my clapping. It was hard to believe he was walking across the stage into the next chapter of his life. I'd be officially stepping down from the gallery on Monday, leaving Seth solely in charge. It was my graduation gift to him. I couldn't help but smile at the thought of his future. Happiness is complicated, but this was a good day.

* * *

The sun was strong enough to warm my skin beneath my suit coat. I shrugged off the jacket and placed it next to me on the bench. In the distance I could hear Petal and Marc consumed in a fierce game of Frisbee. In the two years since Apollo, Marc had been a constant companion. He was with me in those final months when my eyesight was nearly gone. He was the one who enrolled me on the waiting list for a seeing-eye dog, and now Petal and him were thick as thieves. Sometimes I thought my own dog liked him better than me. If it was true, I didn't mind.

Though the sun shone hotly, there was a cool breeze blowing through the trees of Strawberry Fields. I could hear the leaves rustling above me as two birds departed from their perch and flew off leaving lingering chirps.

"It's a beautiful day, isn't it?" A woman approached the bench where I was sitting.

"Yes, it is. A perfect day."

"Do you mind if I sit with you?"

"Not at all." I moved my jacket from the space next to me.

The woman settled her things on the ground and sat down lightly. She let out a sigh. "It's a shame the world is gray now. I bet today would have had one of the bluest skies."

It's a remark I'm sure was never intended to need a reply, but I provided one anyway. "The world is not the same as it once was, it's true. But I choose to believe there is still beauty in it. Even now, you may not be able to see the yellow sun, but you're stilled warmed by its rays. You may not be able to see the color of the trees, but their soft petals still fall one by one. The beauty isn't lost. It's transformed into something new."

"That's quite poetic."

"It's something my wife would have said." I smiled at the memory of her ever-enduring optimism. Only recently had I found the ability to think about her, more recently still had those thoughts been fond ones. Now, her memory finally brought me joy rather than heartache.

"She must have been a wise woman. What else would she have said?" The woman ended her question with a giggle, almost as if she was part of an inside joke I didn't understand.

"Oh, probably something along the lines of, don't let the past take control of your future. Live your life on your own terms. She sometimes had a knack for sounding like a greeting card."

We shared a brief laugh before another breeze whipped through the air and with it carried the smell of the perfume from the woman next to me. The scent was familiar. It struck a forgotten chord in my heart. I knew it immediately. My face must have betrayed my inner thoughts because at that moment the woman spoke.

"Hello, Killian. It's been a while."

"Tess." A whisper was all I could muster. My voice hitched in my throat, preventing me from saying any more.

"When you're ready, come find me. There's so much you need to know."

I listened to her gather her things and stand. Her shadow shaded me against the warm beams of the sun. She stood for a moment and gave a final word of parting, "You should also know, you have a daughter. One day she'll want to meet you."

I sat paralyzed by shock and listened to the rhythmic tapping of her shoes as they grew quieter and farther away. As I breathed in the words she said to me, their implication came out in a sudden gasp. I jolted back to life and frantically looked around out of habit, desperate that I may find some clue to where she had gone. But of course, the world remained dark, along with her answers. My head longed to prove what my heart already for truth—my story is far from over.

About the Author

Jessie George grew up in Columbus, Ohio. While *I'll Remember You in Red* is her first novel, she's no stranger to her words being read across the country. She's been published in the Journal of Interactive Advertising and works professionally as a copywriter. She lives in Minneapolis, Minnesota with her husband and two cats.

9 798218 854942